THE FALCON CHRONICLES: BOOK ONE

TIGER WARS

STEVE BACKSHALL

Orion
Children's Books

First published in Great Britain in 2012
by Orion Children's Books
Paperback edition first published in Great Britain in 2013
Reissued 2014 by Orion Children's Books
a division of the Orion Publishing Group Ltd
Orion House
5 Upper St Martin's Lane
London WC2H 9EA
An Hachette UK Company

1 3 5 7 9 10 8 6 4 2

ISBN 978 1 4440 1448 8

Printed in Great Britain by Clays Ltd, St Ives plc

For the two neglected Jos in my life, my sister and my agent. Even if I sometimes forget to say it, I'm very lucky to have you both on my side!

He should not kill a living being, nor cause it
   to be killed, nor should he incite another to kill.
Do not injure any being, either strong or weak
   in the world.

Sutta Nipata II,14

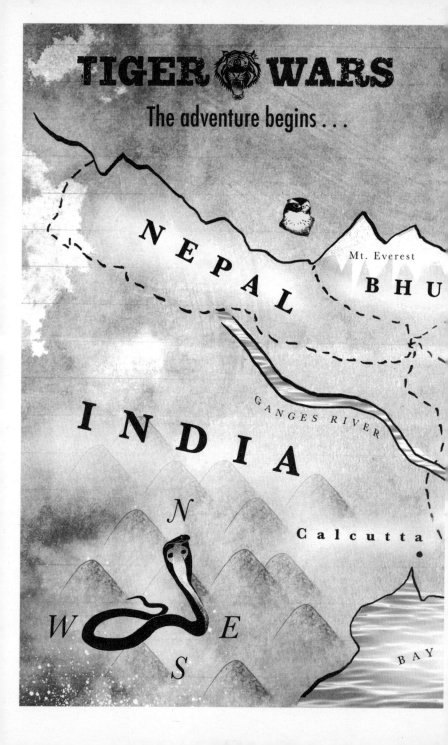

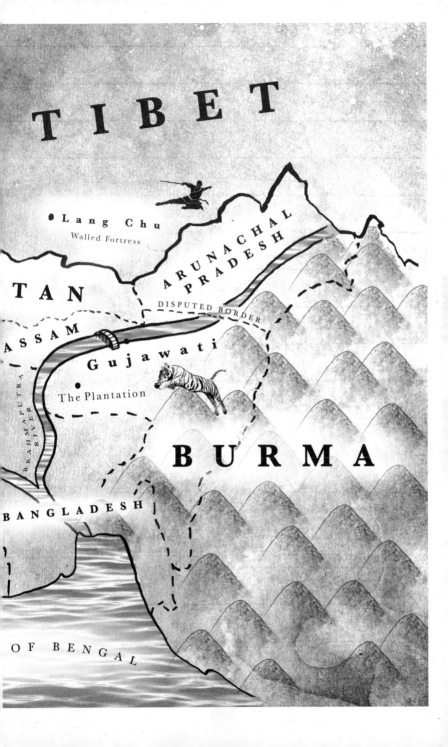

PROLOGUE

The Clan moved through the undergrowth in a silent wave, tuned so finely to each other's movements that communication was barely necessary. They were clearly human but glided as effortlessly as a pack of hunting dogs, with a gait that was neither tiptoeing nor running. Not a single crunch of dry leaves or crackle of broken twigs marked the passing of their bare feet. Every minute or so, one of them would stop and cock his head, listening intently to the tales told by an alarm-calling bird, or to mark the prevailing direction of the meagre wind. They inhaled shallow breaths through their noses, drawing in scents and odours. The sense of smell is one that most humans have simply forgotten to tune, but remains plenty potent enough to track by when it's trained. Each clan member was a boy in his early teens, hair closely cropped, torso sinuous like bunched coils of hemp rope, eyes alert. They took on a loose arrowhead formation. At their apex was a boy of commanding presence, his broad shoulders moving fluidly over his narrow waist, his eyes icy blue like a young wolf pup. He stopped with an abruptness that instantly brought his companions up short, then dropped to his knees to probe the leaf litter. The Clan crowded around him, their movements excited and agitated. The boy called Wolf brushed the leaves aside and revealed a large blocky twist of black dung, as sticky and pungent as newly slicked tar. Tiger scat, and it was fresh! The Clan practically yipped and yelped, pleading to be unleashed. Wolf nodded. They splintered, and leapt forward at a sprint.

The one known as Saker ran with an easy loping stride. It was all he could do to stop from yelling with excitement as he chased the invisible story left by the mighty predator. Saker's long bow was strapped tightly to his shoulders, but still bounced awkwardly with his biggest leaps, threatening to catch on low branches as he passed. Instead of stopping and stooping below such obstacles, he'd barely break stride, but drop to the ground and bound effortlessly like a macaque dashing between trees. He stopped dead. Ahead in a thicket something was out of place. Light pierced through the trees creating slats of orange and white brightness and black shadow . . . in such coloured light, the striped cat was almost invisible. Almost. Its amber eyes gave it away, staring intently at Saker, watching his every move. Gently, fluidly, trying not to breathe, Saker took the bow from his back. It was an ash longbow, much like medieval marksmen once used, but it was certainly not a primitive tool. Saker knew it could take down a deer at fifty paces, and the tiger was much closer. He notched an arrow into the string and drew the fletches back, the bowstring grazing his cheek. As he pointed the arrowhead at his mark, the tiger hissed with fury, flattened its ears against its head and sprang. The undergrowth yielded a massive form, one which moved with explosive and irresistible power, mouth open, vast canine teeth yellow against the dark of its gullet. Saker didn't flinch. He unleashed the arrow, and the tiger fell. Heart thumping, Saker released his pent up breath, levelled his bow with a new arrow already held in trembling fingers, and moved forward cautiously. There is nothing more dangerous than a wounded and cornered predator. He soon saw that there was no danger. The tiger lay on its side, breathing with shallow fast breaths. The arrow shaft protruded from its chest, and with every heave of its breast, a glug of blood flooded from the entry wound. Its eyes weren't shut yet, but soon would be. Saker crept closer, drawing his knife to finish the majestic beast off. It needed to be clinical so the coat wouldn't be damaged. As he knelt, he inhaled the musky pungent smell of big beast, and the tiger looked up at him with golden eyes. It almost seemed to be pleading, imploring. Saker lifted his knife, then stiffened. There was something else in the bushes. Creeping over the tigress, he moved the brush aside. Before him were two small, mewing cubs, their eyes barely open, shrinking into the cover and trying to make themselves invisible. It was as if he had been punched in the chest. Something was very, very wrong with this. Saker shook his head. They were another prize, part of the contract. He had done well.

But no . . . clouds were clearing in his brain . . . how could this be right? The animal before him was one of the brethren, a near-sacred beast. He looked down at her heaving flanks. The arrow wound was fatal, but it would not be swift. The thought of her suffering was overwhelming. Gritting his teeth, he gripped the handle of his blade and lifted it high.

1

He came to as if someone had just thrown a bucket of ice water in his face, gasping for breath, shocked into a sudden brilliant consciousness. Nostrils filled with the heavy smell of dead wet leaves, he lifted his head to see dense trees forming a cavern around him. Slightly muffled by the trees and away in the distance was the sound of excited barking dogs, following a scent, drawing closer. His combat trousers and sodden cotton tunic were drenched with sweat, and . . . was that blood? Yes, it was, thick blood almost black around his stomach, but he felt no pain. Perhaps it wasn't his blood? His head hurt though, with a fierce sharp pain that focused his concentration. He looked down and studied his hands. They belonged to a boy in his early teens, with sparse fine black hair on the forearms, and damp earth rammed deep beneath the fingernails. The hands looked strong though, with calloused knuckles and prominent veins, the hallmarks of hard work. He ran his fingers through his hair, probed the swollen part of his skull, and wincing, looked at his hand again. His palm was red with fresh blood, and this time he was certain it was his own. Instantaneously he found himself relaying a status report. "Impact trauma, I was probably struck with a blunt instrument, there's swelling and a thumb-length open wound, moderate danger of internal bleeding and concussion." Head wounds always bleed profusely he told himself, and in this humid forest he would have to be very careful about infection. The gash would certainly have to be cleaned and stitched.

That could wait, though, while he tried to work out what the hell was going on. He'd been taught that it's quite common to wake up in an unfamiliar place after a deep sleep or perhaps a general anaesthetic and not know where you are for a few seconds. This sensation quickly disappears as the brain catches up, and the recent past comes rushing back. But this wasn't what was happening. And worse, not only did he have no idea where he was, or how he came to be there, he had no clear memories at all. There was just a wispy notion of slats of light playing orange, black and white on the forest floor, and a pungent scent, lingering in his nostrils. What was his name? Not even that sprang to his lips. But then his mind played back a short piece of film, tall boys with cropped hair, stripped to the waist to show their dangerous-looking physiques, faces cruel, lips curled in snarls. "Saker, Saker," they chanted. A sudden recollection. He reached down to his

6

ankle and pulled up his left trouser leg. There on his calf was a bite mark, no blood but still white, and inflicted by blunt teeth. Below it, above his ankle, was a simple monochrome tattoo, the head of a hook-beaked bird of prey, the huge eye dark and intimidating. A saker falcon. Yes! Saker was his name; that at least made sense. The distant barking of the dogs shook him out of this small triumph. With sudden clarity he knew they were tracking him, and they were getting closer. He listened intently for a few seconds. "Four dogs, two German Shepherds, a Dobermann, and . . . one more, I'm not sure . . ." He guessed from the way the calls penetrated the undergrowth that they were just over a kilometre away. The dogs would be coursing, noses close to the ground to suck on the trail he'd left behind, able to pick up the tiniest of scents with a sense of smell many thousand times more potent than that of a human. Drenched with sweat and blood, he would make ludicrously easy tracking fodder. Quickly calculating how distant the barks seemed, he worked out that they would be here in under six minutes.

Something primal in the back of his brain was telling him to run.

As Saker got to his feet and his perspective changed, he realised that he was not alone. Lying face-down in the leaf litter was a man, big, over six feet tall and built like a nightclub doorman, with no neck to speak of and huge shoulders. He was dressed in black combat fatigues from head to toe, with a bullet-proof vest over the top.

"Private security . . ." Some macho tough nut who did a lot of weights, ate too many burgers and loved looking mean in his uniform. Potentially dangerous, no reason to risk waking him . . . but then curiosity overcame common sense, and Saker grabbed one of the black-clad meaty shoulders, and rolled the figure onto his back. He was unconscious, and the bruising round his throat and his contorted face made it clear that he had been choked. Saker had another flash of memory, and saw the big man staggering around, a berserk figure riding his shoulders, wrists locked around the massive throat, crushing the arteries that feed blood to the brain and cutting off the windpipe at the same time. The frenzied figure was pushing down with his legs onto the big man's shoulders, using his whole body to get extra leverage. Clawing at his throat in desperation as he started to black out, the man sank his teeth into the calf muscle of his tormentor. In Saker's mental flashback, the view flew from the struggling security guard, and zoomed up to his shoulders and in on the face of his assailant. Everything came in to focus. Saker was looking at his own face, twisted with effort and fear. Well, that explained the bite mark on his leg. As the big man dropped, he'd taken Saker with him. Their combined weight had meant that they'd come down like a felled oak tree. The gash in his forehead must have been caused by him clattering into a rock that was sticking up out of the leaves. He was lucky to have got away with just a cut. Looking down at his hands again, Saker's head began to spin; the security guard's meaty paws were twice the size of his.

"How could I possibly have overpowered this big lump?" He was suddenly frightened, and shivered despite the humidity. What was he doing here all alone, fighting a big man in this foreign forest? He cocked his head to one side, and stood perfectly still. The normal sounds of the forest had silenced, the birds had stopped singing as they sensed the approaching dogs. A few hundred metres off, a short whistle repeated three times; a spotted deer's alarm call. The deer might as well have been shouting, "They're coming for you".

There was no time to search the body for further clues. Saker turned away from the noise of the baying dogs and ran.

2

Sinter looked in the mirror and saw a very unhappy girl looking back. The kohl outlining her eyes had smeared her cheeks, and some of the dark makeup had dripped onto her saffron-coloured sari. She sat at the vanity table in her bedroom, two large fans circulating the air above her, the room dominated by a four-poster bed draped with muslin mosquito nets. Her almond-shaped eyes were an unearthly amber colour, and were often likened to those of an imperial tigress, but today they were red with tears. Hers was the face of a child of privilege, used to getting exactly what she wanted. As a high-caste Brahmin from a wealthy family, Sinter was privately schooled, and was encouraged not to have any contact with the lesser castes of Indian society. That had always seemed wrong to her. When the tea-pickers on her father's estate greeted her with "Namaste", Sinter was supposed to avert her eyes and pretend to be engrossed in her book, or to have noticed something interesting elsewhere. This was how things were in the foothills of the Indian Himalayas. The technological revolution rampaging across India had, in many places, swept aside centuries-old barriers of class and rank. In modern India, anyone was theoretically capable of making their fortune, and old money was no longer a guarantee of security. However, here in the Northern state of Assam where India met the mighty Himalayas, things were yet to change. Most of the tea was still taken from her father's estate in carts drawn by two sturdy bullocks, and would take days to reach the sellers in Gujawati city, where perhaps the world's largest tea auction house was situated. Troops of Golden Langur monkeys chased over the tumbledown rock walls of the estate as the sun faded, scolded away from the freshly made bundles of tea leaves by the pickers as they finished their day's work. At dusk after her governess allowed Sinter to put her studies aside, one of the house-girls would draw her a cooling bath in a huge old wrought iron tub. They'd add rose petals and jasmine, stirring the water slightly so that the flowers appeared to dance on the surface of the bath. Through the windows of the bathroom, she could look out beyond the tea plantation to the mountains turning brown, grey, then black as the sun set. Yes, you could certainly say that Sinter was someone used to getting exactly what she wanted in life.

Until today. It was to be her fifteenth birthday within

a fortnight, and when her father had ordered her to come down to the conservatory in her best sari, she'd half-wondered if it was part of some grand birthday plan, or perhaps an early present he had waiting for her. She was met by her father and a rotund man wearing a generous white suit. He was in his middling years, and rather shorter than Sinter. The plump man beamed graciously, held out his hand, and introduced himself as Doctor Arjun. Already aware of the expectations of someone in her position, Sinter immediately took on the role of highborn hostess. She spoke with confidence and a charm that had the good doctor turning quite red in the cheeks.

"I am very pleased to make your acquaintance, Doctor Arjun. We so rarely get visitors who are prepared to come this far."

"Doctor Arjun and I have had business dealings for many years now, Sinter," her father responded, clearly proud of his daughter's performance. "He is a very reputable man, with an estate in the Hessam Valley." Hessam was perhaps forty miles to the south of their home, though Sinter had never been there. Her father had an old car, but rarely used it as the roads were so awful that it would have taken the best part of a day to get there.

Doctor Arjun took up the story. "Yes, it is certainly nothing compared to your own home."

Sinter nodded graciously, as if to say she was sure that was not true.

The doctor continued. ". . . And we, of course, do not

grow tea, my practice has me far too busy for a plantation life. However, we do have a small orchard . . . the mango trees are quite wonderful when they are in season."

Again Sinter smiled politely, but she was starting to wonder where all this was going.

"I understand that you had dreams of becoming a doctor yourself when you were a child!" Arjun said, chuckling.

Sinter laughed along with him, but with less enthusiasm now. Actually, she felt rather indignant. She hadn't given up her idea of being a doctor; why should it be so funny or childish that she should even think of it? And who was this round little man that he felt free to laugh at her dreams?

"Perhaps you will be able to watch me in my work some time; the work can be very interesting, you know."

Sinter's amber eyes flicked to her father. What was going on? Her father was staring into his lap and didn't meet her gaze.

"Yes, we think you will be very happy," continued Arjun. "You can bring your governess with you if you wish, and then when you reach the required age, we will be married in accordance with the law."

"What?" Sinter leapt out of her chair as if she'd been stung by a hornet.

"Married?! Are you crazy? Papaji, what is he saying, this man is as old as you are!"

"Sinter, sit down." Her father was firm, angry even.

13

Sinter flinched, she wasn't accustomed to him speaking to her like this. "This has been decided. Doctor Arjun is a respectable man, you will not talk this way in front of him."

"But I don't even know him!"

"There will be many years for that," said Arjun.

"I don't *love* him," she pleaded.

"What does that have to do with it?" Doctor Arjun seemed slightly mystified. Her father, though, looked red in the face, and fit to burst with anger and embarrassment.

"My apologies, Doctor, she clearly hasn't grown up as much as her governess had promised." Then to her, "Sinter, you may leave us now, we have much to talk about." It was not a request. It was an order.

For the first time in her life, Sinter was totally at a loss. She stood there in her best sari, her face burning with shame and fury, impotent under the weight of what she had heard. A whole lifetime of possibilities and ambitions had just crumbled to nothing around her ears.

In the sanctity of her room, Sinter tied her long black hair up with a tortoiseshell clip, and wiped her tears and runny eye makeup away with cucumber water. She felt so stupid. Of course in this part of India arranged marriages were still the norm, but she had always assumed things would be different for her. She was a modern Indian, she knew about computers and technology. She wanted a career and to make her own choices, not to become a servant to a man she didn't even know. She'd never dreamed that she could be destined for this.

14

It wasn't the first tragedy in her life, but her mother's death had come when she was still too young to really grieve. Her father had always remained rather distant, but he'd given her everything she'd asked for. Naively, Sinter had taken this for love. But how could he love her, if he was prepared to sell her off as part of a business deal? Sinter thought back over the years for something that might prove her father's affection. Suddenly his insistence that she look her best whenever there was company took on sinister undertones. And her governess, who'd trained her to be the perfect lady, perhaps she had done that so Sinter would ultimately fetch a good bride price. She'd assumed her father was proud of her, and wanted her to succeed, but now she could only think that she'd been nothing more than an investment.

Unwinding the cloth of the sari, she changed into her bathing costume, and pulled on some jeans. On the far side of the estate where the tea-covered hills met the forests was Sinter's favourite place: a bathing hole surrounded by a tangle of trees and ferns, overhung with lianas and sheltered from the fierce sun even at midday. It was where Sinter went whenever she needed to clear her head and think. It was where she wanted to be right now.

One of the tea pickers, a girl about her own age called Anjali, had shown it to her as a thank you. Sinter had seen that Anjali's hands were blistered from days of work, and had dressed Anjali's palms with muslin and a poultice of tea leaves and lavender oil. Sinter's father would have been furious if he'd known she was fraternising with the workers, let alone treating their ailments. But, to Sinter, seeing Anjali's infected hands lose their angry red colour and heal was probably the most exciting, rewarding thing she'd ever done. Ever since, she'd taken great pride in helping the workers with their minor medical problems, dressing superficial wounds or offering herbal remedies for tummy troubles and mild fevers. The pickers were "Sudras" caste, and Assamese society would only allow them to be labourers. Though not as lowly as the outcast "untouchables", they had no access to medicines, and had not built up any resistance to them. Because of that, the effects of modern drugs were far more potent. Half an aspirin would give them pain relief they thought close to miraculous.

Once, Sinter had eaten dinner with Anjali and her family. They lived in the small shantytown on the edge of the estate that was home to all the workers. The family sat on the floor of their open veranda, eating rice and vegetables with their fingers. "Kum-Sinter, you do us a great honour by eating with us," Anjali's father had said, using the prefix "Kum" to show respect. Sinter was embarrassed. It didn't seem fitting for a man who was the same age as her father to be kowtowing to her. She bowed her head to show it was not necessary. She also knew that the family could ill-afford to be giving her extra food.

"Not at all, sir, thank you so much for your kind invitation. If there is anything I can do to help your family with medicine, you must please let me know."

They'd replied with downcast eyes; despite their poverty they would almost certainly be too proud to ask for her help. After the simple dinner Anjali had led Sinter through the estate and through the forest to the bathing hole.

"We will never be able to thank you, Kum-Sinter, for your help. I'm sure your father would be very angry if he knew you were coming here."

There was so much that wasn't said in that sentence, but Sinter knew Anjali was absolutely right. Her father would have been furious. He would have said this was beneath them, that she was bringing shame on their name. Sinter hadn't told Papaji she was coming to dinner, and knew she'd have to force down another meal later on to cover her tracks. But it was worth it.

Though she'd been given many simple gifts for her healing help, the introduction to the waterhole was the best present. Macaque monkeys with their guilty-looking red faces would come down to the waterside when the langurs weren't around to boss them about. She often saw sambar deer drinking at the pool, sometimes mighty stags with hefty antlers, other times the more delicate hinds with their fawns tottering alongside, trying to hide behind their mother's flanks. She felt so at home here, the place seemed to be bursting with life and there was always some new surprise waiting for her at the waterside. Almost every day she would run back to the house breathless, to go through Papaji's encyclopedias and try to learn the identity of some strange bug or gloriously coloured bird.

Some years back Sinter's waterhole had seen high drama, when a huge paw print was found in the mud there. From side to side it was as wide as Sinter's head, and consisted of a large pad mark, then four round toe prints with no visible claw marks left behind . . . a tiger! It had come down to the pool either to drink or to stalk sambar deer, and might well be back. She could remember the thrill of tracing the deep shape of the print there in the mud, imagining the mighty tiger prowling silently, claws retracted into the pads to keep them sharp. Every print was deeper than Sinter could press her fingers – he must have been so heavy!

Tigers were seen so rarely. Sinter knew that just a hundred years ago India had over one hundred thousand tigers, and people had very real reason to be afraid of the forests. Ever since, though, they had been hunted with such intensity that there were probably no more than fifteen hundred tigers left in the whole of the country, and most of those in small national parks that were little more than big zoos.

People had only recently realised quite how dire the situation was in India's national parks, because *recorded* numbers of tigers had been steadily growing for decades. Everyone thought that tiger numbers were perfectly healthy. Then some bright spark in a conservation charity had pointed out that the Indian government had been rewarding national park authorities if their tiger numbers increased, and imposing severe penalties if they decreased. Not surprisingly, those in charge of the parks had been fiddling the figures for years. A new estimate by an independent organisation revealed the sad news that there were actually less than half as many tigers living in India.

So the chances of ever coming face to face with a tiger here were minuscule. Even so, after the track was found Sinter's father had put the waterhole out of bounds to his workers, little knowing his daughter spent so much time there.

But Sinter didn't feel like obeying her father's orders. "And if I do get mauled by a tiger," she thought, "then they'll all be sorry!"

Saker had been running through the forest for about twenty minutes. He was tall for his age, and ran with an easy, long stride, taking care never to lapse into a sprint that would tire him too quickly. He calculated that unless he took an additional injury, he could continue at this pace without rest, food or water for about an hour. The fact that the pursuing dogs were barking with such frustrated intensity meant they were on the lead, straining to get on with the chase. If they'd been released, they would have run him down in a matter of minutes.

So they were leashed and being held back by trackers who would only let them loose when in sight of their quarry. This was great news, because it meant that all he had to do was be fitter and faster than the trackers themselves, and even with his head wound, he fancied his chances.

Hard running gives no time to think, you can contemplate nothing more than regulating your breathing and placing each foot so you don't take a tumble. But Saker's mind was alive with questions, half-played nightmare fragments, screaming at him as his lungs burned with the moist air he sucked in.

Who was chasing him? The unconscious security guard had the heavy jaw and features of an Eastern European combat soldier, and had mercenary written all over him, so could be serving a master of any nationality. Actually, that question was probably the least important of all – nobody you'd be happy to see came after you behind snapping attack dogs.

Saker shook the questions away and forced himself to concentrate. Where was he? Well, even this late in the day the temperature was close to thirty degrees, so he was probably quite close to the tropics. That spotted deer call had been familiar, and what was that in the distance . . . the miaowing song of a peafowl . . . they were kept as ornamental birds all over the world, but were native to the Indian subcontinent.

Yes, India! The cotton tunic he wore made sense now.

What on earth was he doing in India?

Despite desperately trying to concentrate on his breathing and his running rhythm, Saker was shocked by a swirl in the mists of his memories. Again it was the dusky form of the tiger that teased him first, but then he saw the circle of boys, who seemed so similar to himself, all with the same short hair, physiques bursting with menacing potential. This time their faces started to morph into monochrome tattoos like his own. A sturdily built boy, with a scarred face and bronze eyes morphed in his mind's eye into the Fossa, a cat-like Madagascan predator that leaps about the tree tops hunting lemurs. Another boy, a slender, quick-moving athlete became Boomslang, a highly venomous snake with the biggest eyes and finest sight of any serpent. And there, standing aloof from the others, bulkier, with big shoulders that almost seemed to float above his waist, and a long scar running across one cheek, was Wolf. For some reason, just picturing him made Saker's stomach leap with fear.

Saker knew he was a part of this group, but he could feel their hatred, and he was suddenly certain: they were his pursuers. But why, and more importantly . . . who was he? All the evidence he had to hand on that question led to places his mind simply didn't want to contemplate. Saker felt as if he knew this forest, the things that lived here and how he could survive in it, but he didn't feel as if he belonged here. Besides, his skin was pale, probably European, and certainly not like any of the peoples native to the Indian subcontinent.

What else . . . well, he was clearly in exceptional physical condition, and if his flashback had been accurate, he'd managed to overpower a mercenary many times his size with his bare hands. And what about his hands? The callouses on the back of the knuckles were like those that martial artists acquire from years of doing press ups on their knuckles to toughen them. So he was a fighter. No surprise there.

Saker stopped dead. He sniffed the air, a familiar, spicy, powerful scent. Tangled around a nearby tree he found exactly what he was looking for: an innocuous-looking vine, with big, broad leaves, and bunches of small green fruits like miniature grapes; peppercorns! Quickly Saker grabbed handfuls of the fruits, old wrinkled ones and new alike. He hunted around for a pair of flat stones, and crushed the peppercorns. Then he spread the pepper across his own footprints, taking care to get as much pepper into his tracks as possible. The black and white pepper used throughout the world all originated from this one Indian plant, and the wild peppercorns still had the potency of the modern spice. It would provide a perfect diversion.

After another six or seven minutes of hard running, Saker splashed down to a small stream perhaps five metres wide and at its very deepest up to his knees. He stooped briefly to scoop some water in his hand, ladling it into his dry mouth, then stopped to listen for a second . . . The dogs' furious barking approached, ever closer. But then came howls, high-pitched wails of canine pain. They had snuffled right into the peppercorn trap he'd left for them.

Tracking dogs run with their noses on the ground, sucking scents into their sensitive nasal cavities where they process the information. Each dog had just sucked in a great noseful of pepper, and as their noses are more effective than humans', they are also more sensitive. Now, far away, Saker could hear sneezing and snorting as the dogs tried to clear their sinuses. They would be useless for quite some time.

He could afford two minutes. He took off his sodden tunic and soaked it in the stream, wringing out as much of the blood and sweat as possible. Twisting the dripping material into a roll, he wrapped it around his neck, so the damp cloth could cool the blood as it passed up his carotid arteries to his brain. *Keep the brain cool and oxygenated, keep the mind clear.* Rapidly giving the rest of his body the once-over, Saker was relieved not to find any other obvious injuries, but he was puzzled by a large white sticking plaster the size of his palm visible above the waistband of his trousers. He felt no sensation of pain beneath it, but just in case it covered an open wound, he decided to leave it be. There was no sense in inviting infection.

The water offered a perfect way to throw the dogs further off the scent. Saker started heading upstream, so his footprints in the shallow water were pointing in that direction, then as soon as he got into deeper water, he lifted his feet off the bottom and floated downstream. The stream wasn't big enough to carry him far, but if he could just get his trackers going in the wrong direction, it would buy him valuable minutes. When he was back in shallow water, he stepped gingerly between submerged rocks, taking care to leave no prints, but also not to slip on the slimy boulders and end up getting injured. Tracker dogs hate water: the tiny scent molecules that cling so insistently to leaves and grass would be carried away in an instant by the flow. Back into the shallows, he took up his easy loping stride, knowing that every step was finally putting distance between him and his pursuers.

Dimly, he became aware of a sandy cliff face cutting across the forest ahead, neatly splicing the stream. That couldn't be right. No, wait, it wasn't a cliff, it was a tumbledown old sandstone wall, probably the boundary to someone's property. It reached to the understorey of the trees, and looked ancient. The stream flowed clean up to the wall and then disappeared, passing through a tunnel to the other side. Saker weighed his options. He could turn away from the stream and follow the wall to the east or the west, looking for an easy place to climb over. He might be able to make it over the top right here, but as this thought crossed his mind, he was struck with a vision of nearing the top, then a chunk of crumbly sandstone coming out in his hands, sending him plummeting to the ground. The thought of lying in the stream, broken, helpless, just waiting for the slavering dogs to find him and tear him apart . . . Saker shuddered. No, a climb would be an unnecessary risk. He visualised the trackers arriving. If they saw damp footprints heading off down the wall they'd be back on his trail, but there was one direction they'd really struggle to follow, and that was to actually go under the wall. Taking a deep breath, he ducked under the water, and pushed himself down into the flow.

S inter made her way through the plantation, plucking some of the finest tips as she walked and chewing on them. They tasted bitter, but were the most valuable part of the tea bush and said to be extremely good for you. Papaji took so much care over his tea, how it was prepared and served. The pot should never be stirred, or the tea leaves squeezed out after they had been given time to brew (the precise time varied depending on the type of tea), and it should only ever be served from fine china. He would become apoplectic if their rare visitors requested milk or sugar with their tea – "Why not just go the whole way and pour in yak butter and salt like the Tibetans?" he'd sneer after they left.

Sinter couldn't feign the same enthusiasm as her father, even if it was the most popular beverage in the world. But though she could take or leave tea, she did adore the plantations. The lines of tea bushes hugged the naturally hilly landscape, providing a carpet of uniform height and colour. In between them, the pickers in their brightly-coloured orange and saffron saris wended their way, chatting gaily to each other. They carried woven baskets in the smalls of their backs, supported by a cloth strap across their foreheads.

On one of her illicit wanders in the tea fields, Sinter had once asked if she could try to lift one of these baskets. An old lady with an enormous ring through her nose connected by a chain to her earring, had given her a massive smile and passed the basket to her. Sinter had not even been able to get it onto her back. That had caused gentle hysterics among the workers, but Sinter didn't feel the slightest mockery from them, and laughed with them.

The pickers held the basket on their backs all day long using just the strength of their neck muscles. As they chatted, they'd pluck the choicest leaves and throw them over their shoulders into the baskets. Above them, black and brahminy kites would circle, ever-watchful birds of prey hoping to spot any rodents or large bugs spooked out of the bushes by the women as they worked.

Now, as Sinter walked among the workers, there was no way she would let them see that she'd been crying. The last thing she wanted was their sympathy, or even to talk about what had happened. She'd carefully cleaned her face, and wore a determined if not happy expression, smiling to those she recognised as she strolled towards the waterhole. On the inside she was utterly miserable. This was her home, these were her friends, it was all she had ever known and where she truly belonged. Here she was never lonely. When the pickers had returned to their huts on the edge of the estate, she had the langurs and the macaques for company, the jewelled frogs that called to each other on rainy nights, even the cobras and kraits that slithered about the plantation in search of rodent prey held no fear for her. To Sinter, every day held new wonders, and in the natural world she had a school and a playground that she would never tire of. For the moment at least, she forced herself to avoid thinking about how all of this was soon to disappear from her life.

At the far end of the estate was an area of hillside too steep and irregular in shape to have been any use in tea planting, so the trees there had never been felled, and it remained a sizeable chunk of woodland, merging with the vast forest beyond the estate walls that ran all the way to the foothills of the Himalayas. A small sandy path wound into the trees and down to the water. As she approached, several bright blue and turquoise birds took off from their perches at the waterside – rollers, or blue jays, common but dazzling birds.

Crouching in the silty sand, Sinter prepared to strip to her bathing costume, but was stopped by a rustle in the bushes on the other side of the pool. Tiny beads of sweat sprang up on her forehead, and a prickly sensation tingled up the back of her neck. She was suddenly certain that she was being watched. Ever so slowly she looked up.

Across the water from her in the bushes, a dark shape, and two eyes stared straight at her.

Her first impulse was to turn and run, but then she remembered. After she had healed Anjali's hand, Anjali's father had talked to her about big cats. "If you are ever faced with a tiger, don't ever run. *Prey* runs. Deer run, buffalo run, monkeys run. If you run from the tiger, you will trigger his deepest hunter's instincts, he will come for you even if that was not his original intention . . . and you can never outrun the tiger."

Sinter had nodded seriously as Anjali's father continued with his instructions: "You must stand tall and strong, face him so he knows he cannot stalk you any closer. Tell him that you see him and that you are not afraid." With tears in her eyes, she remembered herself as a young girl nodding solemnly at his wisdom, promising him she would do as he said. How different it was now to be faced by the threat for real. Raising herself up to her full height, Sinter stood stock still staring into the bushes.

"I see you," she said. "My father is coming to find me soon with his gun . . . and I am not afraid of you."

As she stood trembling, the bushes parted, and the silent watcher stood up and faced her.

Sinter flinched instinctively, having prepared herself for a pouncing tiger, then let out a huge sigh of relief: it was just a boy, no older than she was.

"I thought you were a tiger!" No sooner had she uttered the words than she felt really stupid. What kind of baby believes that every shadow she sees in the forest is a prowling wild animal? Embarrassed, Sinter felt her pride spiked, and to save face vented her fury on the stranger.

"This is a private estate you know, you can't just walk around here, if my father finds you here you'll be arrested. You know that on some estates round here you could be shot for trespassing?"

The watcher looked singularly unimpressed by her outburst. In fact he seemed to be weighing up something else in his mind as she was speaking; he even looked off into the distance as if listening for something.

She looked at him more carefully. He stood a full head taller than she did, bare-chested and clad only in a pair of combat trousers, barefoot too, and with some kind of scarf round his neck. His nose was strong and thin, almost hooked, and his eyes so dark they appeared to be black. He was soaking wet and breathing heavily. All of a sudden it occurred to Sinter that tigers are not the only dangerous creatures that lurk in bushes. Poachers! Everyone round the plantation knew about the tiger poachers, truly bad men who caught tigers in crude snares, put them through unbelievable suffering, and then killed them. They would sell their beautiful pelts and their body parts to be used in Chinese medicine, and for no more than a few hundred US dollars. These were the men who had brought tigers to the brink of extinction, and some of the national parks operated a shoot-to-kill policy against them. The poachers were always armed, dangerous men, outcasts and outlaws.

Sinter turned and without a second thought ran up the path, screaming for her father.

Saker had seen the girl too late. After tugging his way blind through the submerged tunnel under the sandstone wall, he'd popped to the surface gasping for breath, totally disorientated by the swirl of the flow. He was in another forested glade, but this time it was definitely different. Well-worn footpaths came down to the water's edge, and there were several big earthenware jars lying there, obviously discarded after they had been cracked. Just as Saker was taking this in, he'd become aware of someone approaching, and had swiftly waded out of the water and ducked behind a rhododendron bush. It was nothing like dense enough to hide him, so he had to rely on stillness, and hope the interloper wasn't paying too much attention. When Sinter walked into sight, he softened slightly. A young girl, dressed in modern Western clothes but unmistakably Indian. If only she'd not seen him, if only she hadn't run screaming. But she did. There was no way Saker could risk her giving him away to anyone.

Sinter had a short head start, but he plunged through the stream, and coming up behind her, he tapped her ankle as she ran, like a cheetah clipping the heel of a gazelle. Sinter went down hard, bumping her arm and grazing her knees, crying out in fear and pain. Saker moved swiftly, dropping behind her, clasping his hand over her mouth, pinning her arms around her with his other arm. Try as she might to bite his hand and to struggle free of his grasp, it was impossible, he was too strong.

"Stop fighting, you're not going anywhere, save your strength. OW!" She continued to writhe around, and had just managed to bite his hand.

"OK, if you don't stop struggling I'm going to have to knock you out or something . . . it's your choice, I don't want to hurt you."

She tensed perceptibly, obviously making up her mind, then slackened. Saker waited a few seconds, then took his hand away. Sinter sobbed with fear and fury.

"My father will be down here any second. He knows I'm here, and he has a gun!"

This sounded highly unlikely, and was almost certainly a bluff, but he couldn't take any chances. And if he let her go, she really would run back to her father and create a whole heap more trouble. He had nothing to tie her up with, and really *didn't* want to hurt her. It seemed wrong. There was only one course of action.

"Right, listen to me very carefully. I can't have you running back to your father and giving away where I am, so you're coming with me." He paused and thought some more. "And, you can't slow me down, so you keep up, and you keep quiet. Make a break for it, or shout for help, and . . . and, well, I'll have to do something horrid." He allowed a few seconds for this to sink in. "Now come on!"

Grabbing her firmly by the upper arm, Saker dragged

Sinter through the bushes and into the plantation. Once in the open, he took the dirt track that led away from the buildings and towards the main gate that was the only real entrance and exit to the estate. As they ran, the plantation workers looked up and shouted, "Hey, it's little Doctor Sinter!", "Where are you going?", "What's going on?". Sinter was too busy gasping for breath to answer.

But ahead was something the poacher boy had not counted on. At the gate, Tariq, the security guard would be waiting. He was a huge Sikh, with a great moustache that he used to wear in a sort of net hammock at night to keep it trim. Ever since Sinter had been a child she'd been afraid of him, and considered him to be the most frightening man she'd ever known. He carried an ancient Lee Enfield rifle, slung proudly over his shoulder, and would interrogate everyone who came in or out of the plantation. Tariq would soon put a stop to this madness. There was the gate in front of them now, and Tariq standing in the small guardroom. His attention was caught as the couple sprinted down to the gate, and picking up his rifle he leapt to his feet. Sinter saw that he had been in the process of combing his incredibly long black hair, which as with all Sikhs is never cut, and had not had a chance to put his turban back on again. She had never seen him without the turban before, and was sure he would be livid that she had now. This boy had no idea what he was getting himself into.

"STOP! What is the meaning of this, Sinter?" As Tariq

strode out from the guardhouse, he clearly intended to give Sinter the dressing down of a lifetime. But then he saw the boy's bloodied head, the way his fingers seemed to pinch right into Sinter's flesh, and the terrified look on her face, and Tariq's manner abruptly changed. He swung the Enfield from behind his back and into his hands, and drew back his chin into his most imperious stance, a blockade as impressive as the gate itself.

Saker didn't so much as break stride. He maintained all the momentum of his charge, then at the last second skidded along the grass feet first. One foot went in between Tariq's legs, the other outside them, then he scissored them together with incredible force. Tariq crashed to the ground, banging his head as he went down. Saker leapt on him, and drove the heel of his hand into the big Sikh's stomach, driving the wind out of his lungs. Then he was back on his feet. He had only let go of Sinter's arm for a matter of seconds. Dragging her on, Saker rammed into the gates with his shoulder, and they bounced open.

Ahead lay a twisting road bordered on one side by the forest, and on the other by fields full of cows and crops. The road itself had once been tarmacked by a local government filled with ambition, but they'd not had the funds to maintain it. Scorching summers and a hundred thousand hooves had battered it until it was about as navigable as the surface of the moon.

Sinter was pulled along with fear rising in the back of her throat. Who was this boy? And then she became aware

34

of another noise beyond the panicked breathing of her own burning lungs. Dogs. Dogs barking frantically in the distance. She noticed Saker flick a glance over his shoulder. He looked like a hunted man. He was being chased! All she had to do was slow him down, and whoever was chasing would catch him and she'd be safe. She deliberately caught her foot on a stone, and tumbled into the dirt, taking Saker with her.

"That wasn't very smart," Saker growled as he scrambled to his feet.

"What? I tripped, I can't keep up with you, you should leave me!"

"You knew exactly what you were doing," Saker said, nodding in the direction of the dogs, "and if you knew what was chasing us, you wouldn't be helping them."

He shook his head, shaking away mental cobwebs. How did he know the pursuers were the bad guys? Maybe *he* was the bad guy! After all, he had already attacked two men and kidnapped this girl – those were not exactly the actions of a hero. And she was slowing him down. Maybe he should just leave her here in the dirt? But then he reasoned that having a hostage gave him a few more cards, a bit of bargaining power. He grabbed her arm again.

"Go down one more time, and I'll take your shoes and make you run barefoot too."

Sinter shrieked as she was yanked to her feet and off down the road once more.

Abruptly, the barking behind them went from muffled

to spectacularly clear. Back at the wall of the plantation, the dogs had broken clear of the forest and were on the road. They were specks in the distance, but Saker saw them. "Two German Shepherds, a Dobermann and . . . a Ridgeback. Great."

Rhodesian Ridgebacks were sandy-coloured African dogs bred for hunting lions. Four bulky men in dark uniforms the same as the mercenary led the dogs, and alongside them . . . Saker gasped. Three tall boys, rangy, sinuous, with identical short, almost shaven, hair, all breaking into a sprint on the potholed road.

They were no more than four hundred metres away. The forest offered no security any more. He could plunge back into its cover, but then they could just unleash the dogs, and they would be on him in no time.

Think, you idiot, think!

4

As the words left his lips, the black-clad men reached for the collars of their charges and set them loose. The dogs leapt forward and sprinted towards their goal like the hounds of hell unleashed. Saker stopped, turned and stood his ground. There was no sense in running now. Taking his tunic from round his neck, he wrapped it around his forearm. He could at least take one dog on his arm and maybe wrestle it to the ground before they all fell on him. But then there was a new noise, a nostalgic tooting like something from an old Western movie. Sinter couldn't quite believe what she was hearing. The old train line that ran through the fields to one side of the road only had a train trundle down it about once a week, so for one to come by now was the most bizarre twist of fate. Or fortune. But then, as she looked towards the charging dogs, she suddenly had a cold feeling tickle down the back of her neck.

"Listen to me," Saker said, "these dogs don't know the difference between me and you, they're just trained to kill. Either you run with me, or you take your chances with them."

She had less than a second to make up her mind, and when Saker tugged her into the field, Sinter didn't resist. In fact, she almost overtook him as they raced towards the train.

It was an old-fashioned steam train, churning gobbets of black smoke from the smoke stack of its engine, the front few carriages crammed full of people, sweetmeat vendors and passengers hanging out of every carriage. The rear two carriages were open-sided stock cars with sliding doors. As they sprinted towards the tracks Sinter could see the shadowy faces of stowaways inside.

Suddenly there was an excited yip behind them as the dogs drew close. She didn't dare look back. They reached the doorway in the last stock car as it threatened to trundle past. Though the train looked as if it was going at a snail's pace, that was misleading, and it was actually travelling at quite a lick. Sinter couldn't believe what was happening – they were trying to jump on to a moving train! Saker went first, leaping onto the wooden floorboards inside the stock car, folding the top of his body over into the car, then swinging his legs up to follow. He immediately turned to help Sinter, but the train was going too fast. She couldn't catch it, she wasn't tall enough to make the leap that he had. Sinter stumbled, felt the hot breath of a dog on her neck, and then a brutal grip took the back of her shirt collar and tugged her off her feet.

A pair of jaws snapped shut with a horrifying "click" behind her, as Sinter found herself sprawling on the floor of the stock car. The dogs kept pace alongside the train, barking furiously and leaping at the open side, the Dobermann even managing to catch hold of the side and struggling to get on board, but slipping back down with a yelp. As the tireless train slowly left the dogs behind, Sinter looked up through teary eyes and sobs at Saker, who had certainly saved her life. He was standing in the doorway staring back down the tracks.

"So what now?" she sobbed. "You're kidnapping me? Where are you taking me? And what are you going to do to me?"

She said it as much for the ears of the silent stowaways, sitting in the half light, who hadn't commented on the invasion of their hiding place. They were thin, drawn men, possibly beggars, unlikely to be of any use to her, but somehow she wanted them to hear her anyway.

"You are free to go," Saker responded impassively. "Next time this train stops, you can get off. Well . . . or you could always hop off now, if you're feeling brave."

She looked at the fields rushing by outside the stockcar. She wasn't feeling that brave.

"Who are you? And why were they chasing you?" She stopped and chose her words carefully. "Are you on the run from the police?"

39

"Did they look like police to you?"

He had a point there. Indian police wear blue uniforms, never have attack dogs – at least not out here they didn't – and they were always . . . well . . . Indian.

Saker sat down with his back to the sliding door, knees pulled up to his chest, and scratched his head with both hands. He dropped his chin. For the first time since she'd met him, he didn't look so tough.

"And . . . I'd really like to answer your first question but . . . I don't exactly know who I am."

Sinter looked at him with new interest. "What do you mean?"

Saker breathed in deeply and closed his eyes. He was clearly making up his mind about something. Then he let the breath go. Maybe it would help to get it off his chest; perhaps talking about it would help him find some sense in the insanity. And what harm could it do to tell this girl? He didn't intend to be in her company much longer.

"The only clear memories I have are of the last . . . I don't know, hour or so. I woke up in a forest, with a beat-up guy at my feet, and my head bleeding. I'm pretty sure it was me who beat him up. I'm being chased by some seriously scary people, and I have no idea why but I seem to know loads about staying alive and fighting, though I don't know how. I know that this has something to do with it though." He rolled up his trouser leg to reveal his tattoo.

"What's that?"

"It's a saker falcon. Superb hunters, keen eyesight, they

40

hunt their prey by chasing them down in flat-out flight . . .
I think this is me . . . well, I think it's my name."

It was the craziest thing Sinter had ever heard.

"So you expect me to believe that you've got amnesia?
That you've forgotten who you are? You snatched me from
my home, dragged me for miles . . . you hurt Tariq. You
are a crook, a poacher, you're just a coward who can't
stand what he really is."

"Yeah, maybe. Maybe when I find out what I am, I
won't like it much. But until I've figured it out, you can do
us both a favour . . . and keep your mouth shut."

Saker suddenly became aware of an insistent growling
in his stomach. When mammals are in "fight or flight"
mode, blood is channelled away from the stomach and
other superfluous parts of the body, and taken to the
muscles, the heart, the lungs, the brain – parts where it's
needed most. Saker knew that some animals – even people
– will spontaneously wee themselves when they're frightened.
It might seem gross, but he'd learned that it served a real
purpose, helping to empty the bladder of waste material,
to make a person lighter and make running easier; even to
make themselves more unpalatable to predators. However,
now that Saker was no longer fleeing, he was very aware
that he hadn't eaten for ages, and had consumed an awful
lot of energy in running away. He was starving!

"Have you got any money?" he demanded of Sinter.

She shook her head, but before she could stop him he'd
stuck his hands into her jeans pockets. There wasn't much,

just a few hundred rupees. Saker caught the attention of a small boy who was staring at them both with huge eyes from the gloom. He waved the money and made the universal gesture of pinched hand to mouth that says "I want food". The boy hesitated a second, then grabbed the cash and swung out of the carriage door.

"That's great!" Sinter shouted. "We'll never see that again. That was all I had."

"We'll see," replied Saker confidently.

No more than five minutes later, the boy swung back into the carriage, with a handful of green oranges, a bag of peanuts fried in their shells, and some floury chapattis. Saker nodded, handed the boy a fifty-rupee note, and tucked into the food as if he had never eaten before.

"Huh, shows how much you know," he said to Sinter between mouthfuls of chapatti. "This is supposed to be your country too."

"Am I going to get any of that?" she asked. "It was my money!"

Saker stopped mid-mouthful as if hit by a thought he had simply never had before. He looked at the small haul in his lap, and as if it was causing him physical pain handed over an orange and a chapatti. Sinter was going to retort sarcastically, but stopped herself. She didn't know when she'd next get a chance to eat.

When the food was finished, Saker took his damp tunic from round his wrist, squeezed out the last drops of water, and pulled it on over his head. As he rolled it down to his waistband, he noticed the plaster again. Picking at a corner, he peeled the plaster away to reveal . . . nothing. Nothing at all. The plaster wasn't covering any cut, wound or mark of any kind. That was peculiar. He ran his fingers through his hair and his fingernails caught on the ragged edges of his head wound, making him flinch.

"That needs stitching," said Sinter matter of factly. "A cut like that will get infected out here almost instantly."

Saker rounded on her. "When I want your comments, Florence Nightingale, I'll ask for them."

Sinter was affronted, and not sure why she had cared in the first place.

Outside it was starting to get dark, and the train was heading into the mountains. It would be chilly with the wind rushing through the carriage. Saker picked up a dusty hessian rice sack from the floor and wrapped it around his shoulders. Glancing down at Sinter, who was already beginning to shiver a little, he took another, and offered it to her. She grimaced at him defiantly, but the cold got the better of her, and she took the sack and turned it into a shawl. Sinter's privileged upbringing had never really taken her away from the few other estates close to her father's. With every minute she was getting further and further from her own world, away from Papaji and her governess, away from everything familiar. Looking at Saker, she saw a boy lost in thought yet obviously still fiercely attentive to everything going on around him. He must surely have been exhausted, ready to collapse, yet his eyes didn't flutter, and his head never lolled even slightly with sleep. Instead he stared into the darkness beyond the carriage with dark wide-open eyes like . . . well, like a hawk. She shuddered beneath her rice sack shawl, and this time not only from the cold.

A big bounce and a jolt, and Sinter woke with a stifled scream. It was dawn, and the train was well into the mountains. They were trundling alongside a mirror flat lake, which reflected perfectly the lush mountains behind it. Bright luminous orange light was igniting the tops of the highest green peaks. Their lower slopes were peppered with pine forests, and occasionally Hindu shrines, white stony monoliths painted with red and gold and surrounded by lines dangling flags of every colour imaginable. For a second she was so overcome by the beauty of the view that she didn't fully remember where she was, but suddenly the dramatic events of the previous day came flooding back.

Saker was still sitting in the same position, his back against the door, legs pulled in to his chest. He rested his forehead on his knees, and his eyes were closed. He was asleep. Sinter carefully dropped the sack shawl from her shoulders and looked out at the lake. The train tracks were on an elevated bank, which dropped steeply to the water's edge. It was a big jump, and the movement of the train would make it more dangerous, but surely the water would cushion the blow? She carefully got to her feet and tiptoed to the edge of the carriage. Breathing in deeply, she crouched, ready to throw herself into the wind. Suddenly a hand grabbed her ankle in a grip so powerful it made her wince.

"I hope you've got up to find us some breakfast?" Saker said firmly.

Sinter's tensed shoulders drooped. Her opportunity had gone.

"A jump from a moving vehicle onto uncertain surface is an unnecessary risk, it would almost certainly have broken your leg or worse," Saker stated, as if reading a status report. "I'm sure we'll be pulling into the station soon enough. Enjoy the view, get us some dosas, I don't know, chill out." He dropped his head back onto his knees. "Besides, that lake water would be freezing."

Sinter sat back down on the floor with a sulky shrug. She was again aware of the eyes watching from the darkness, watching her failure and humiliation. She didn't like it one bit. She shivered again in the post-dawn chill. If only she had a jumper, or some socks. Her feet were icy. In the corner of the carriage a pair of travellers were squatting on their heels, hunched around a tiny copper stove, pumping it up with a thin handle to increase the pressure of the fuel inside. It looked as if they were brewing up some tea. Tea! She could almost taste the warming brew right now. She'd have paid a month's allowance for a cup. The travellers noticed her looking over and huddled tighter around their stove, warning her off with their curved shoulders.

"Where is this next stop, then?"

Saker nibbled his bottom lip a bit, and looked out of the door. "I'm not exactly sure. I think we're nearing Arunachal Pradesh, where China is claiming big chunks of India for their own. After that, it's Tibet and the highest mountains in the world."

Sinter started. It sounded so far away from home. Surely she'd be able to find a telephone and call Papaji to come and save her from all of this. Mind you, she'd just be delivering herself back to a future as a glorified servant. Then she bridled slightly at the fact that Saker had seen fit to give her a history lesson about her own country.

"So what's your big plan then?" she demanded.

His shoulders sagged. Once again, he stopped looking like a fierce feral young man, and looked exactly like the boy he really was.

"I don't have a plan. Not a big plan or a little plan. I don't know where I'm going or what I'm going to do."

He sounded so miserable that Sinter's first impulse was to reach out and put her arm around his shoulders, but she drew back instantly. What was she thinking! What he said next, though, made her sit up smartly.

"But I am starting to remember what's going on."

5

The instant the attack dogs returned, doleful and panting, Wolf gave them a piece of his mind. Even the Rhodesian Ridgeback approached on its belly, ears flattened, licking its lips, avoiding eye contact, tail between its legs. He looked as pathetic as it's possible for a dog bred for hunting lions to look.

Any normal human master would probably have melted and been overwhelmed by this show of submissiveness, and would have bent down to ruffle the dog's fur and tell them everything was OK, but Wolf spoke fluent dog. He was the alpha, he was in control of this pack and needed to let them know his displeasure. Wolf opened his mouth to bare his teeth, hissed at the dogs and snarled, standing high and proud above them, aiming a kick towards one of the German shepherds. Ideally, he'd have actually bitten one of them. The dogs retreated, whining, leaving him to watch the train chug slowly off into the mountains. The other humans knew better than to interrupt Wolf while he was thinking.

"You." Wolf pointed to one of the dark-clad security guards, squat and muscular, almost square in appearance. He looked as if he could take out a solid oak door merely by running at it with his head. "Find out where that train stops next."

"Anything else you want?" the guard spat. His tone of voice made it clear that he wanted to add, "If I'm going to be taking my orders from some skinny kid."

Wolf looked at him with disdain. He saw the neckless frame, the soft puffiness of the face that made it look as if the security guard had spent much of his life being punched. He might be handy in an arm wrestle or for bar room thuggery, but all that spare weight was extra baggage.

"Actually, there is something else I want," Wolf replied. "Next time I'd like you to be in better shape, so you don't hold us and the dogs back, and so we catch what we're chasing."

Squat guy huffed and turned away, taking a satellite phone from one of many pockets, holding the aerial high to pick up a signal.

The two other boys gathered close around Wolf now, not speaking, waiting for orders. They seemed like growing cubs, snuffling round the mouth of their wolf mother for her to regurgitate a few scraps for them to eat. One was much smaller than the other, with constant almost agitated movements. With small dark eyes and a slightly upturned nose, he didn't have the threatening demeanour of Wolf. In fact he looked like he'd run for the bushes if Wolf so much as burped. He couldn't sit still, was endlessly twitchy, and looked as if someone had given him too much coffee. Either that, or like a small predator in the weasel family that needed to feed constantly and had to keep moving. He was Polecat. The other was Margay, named after a small, beautiful but fierce spotted cat of Latin America, known for being a superb climber. Margay was also true to his name, possessing a kind of harnessed energy which enabled him at any second to leap into the branches or scamper up a tree trunk. Again, he seemed much more nervous and less sure of himself than Wolf. There was no way *he'd* be snapping orders at the security guards around him.

"Why's he running, Wolf?" asked Margay. "Saker's one of us."

Polecat added, "Where does he think he's going? The Clan are his family."

"Not any more. He's a traitor, and we have to hunt him down like prey," Wolf stated matter of factly. "You'd better get used to that idea, because it might be you that has to finish him."

Margay didn't look as if he liked that idea. His specialty was thieving, climbing in through people's open windows at night while they were sleeping, stealing their secrets away. Saker was stronger than he was, and he knew it.

"Polecat, I need you to contact the rest of the Clan and

bring in some backup. I have to contact the client and let him know we're falling behind schedule." As he spoke, Wolf looked up at the security guys and their dogs. "And tell him that if he wants a job doing properly, he needs to leave it to us, not these muscle-bound mercenaries."

The train rattled on through the mountains. Sinter was curled on the floor of the stock car, wound up in rice sacks, and looked sound asleep. Saker though was far from sleep, with thoughts coursing through his consciousness. The darkness that had been the past was starting to lighten, but far from bringing relief, the remembered snippets held troubling questions. Saker rubbed at the tattoo on his shin as if he expected it to smudge – perhaps it could all prove to be illusory, or a bit of a game. But no, the black ink was permanent. Saker was beginning to remember its significance too.

With all the uncertainty that lay ahead, the last thing he needed was deadwood, a girl slowing him down. Now that she had served her purpose, he had to ditch her at the first opportunity. But something nagged at him. It was almost as if he'd acquired a conscience! He'd dragged her away, put her life at extreme risk, and now taken her miles and miles from home without any way of getting back. In some way he felt responsible for her, and that he had to take care of her. Weirdly, that thought was the first thing that had given him any sense of purpose. And there was something else nagging at him as well. He looked at her shiny dark hair splayed over the dusty wooden floor, and recalled that her almond-shaped amber eyes had a ferocity about them that was . . . well, beautiful. And she had shown such determination, jumping onto the train and standing up to him even when he was threatening her. She was rather more than just deadwood. She was pretty impressive really.

Sinter jolted awake with a start, and opened those amber eyes to see Saker staring at her. Straight away he averted his gaze, feeling self-conscious, though he wasn't sure why. Sinter rubbed her neck, stiff from lying in an awkward position and from the cold.

"Have we stopped yet?" she asked.

"No, it seems to be an overnight long-distance chugger, I reckon it'll stop early this morning. You'll be free of me soon."

Sinter's mouth was dry, and she was chilled to the bone. She would have paid a million rupees for a cup of tea. Saker registered her longing glance towards the travellers at the back of the carriage with their stove. He stood up and walked over to them. Begrudgingly, they relented to the fierce-looking young man and passed Sinter a cup of sweet black tea, which she was so eager to drink she scalded the roof of her mouth. She sat looking at Saker, her palms clasped around the cup, trying to absorb every last morsel of warmth into her body. Saker was still looking at his feet as he began to speak.

"Things started coming back to me last night. Not long after we'd got onto the train, things started to make sense. I don't know, it's almost as if I'd been drugged and it was starting to wear off."

Sinter bit her lip. Something occurred to her. "Maybe it was that plaster you were wearing. I've seen medical compresses that are like that, they just sit on your skin, and drugs that are in the plaster seep through your skin and into your bloodstream over a long time."

"Like a nicotine patch?" Saker asked.

"Exactly, but perhaps the drugs in that plaster were much stronger . . . they made you forget . . . but why would anyone want to make you forget?"

Saker shifted from his sitting position and thought it through. That made so much sense. Things had started becoming clear after he'd removed the plaster, a little after Sinter had slipped into sleep. It was as if he was waking up as she drifted off into blackness. As the minutes went on, a blanket of fog seemed to lift from his consciousness, and the nightmares that had tormented him started to form into people, places and memories.

"Of course . . . they must have put it on me because I was starting to . . . well, because it all started to seem wrong to me, they needed something to control me."

"Who's *they*?" asked Sinter, confused. "You're getting way ahead of yourself, can't you rewind a bit more?"

Saker huffed, thought about it for a second, then made up his mind. He would tell her. This conversation might take a while.

"We are the Clan," said Saker. "Well, I guess I should say 'they' are the Clan."

The Clan was all he knew. When his memories had started to regain reality rather than just being a nightmare, it was the Clan that was the first thing that made sense, and nothing else in his whole life seemed to have happened without them.

"I don't really know when it started, but the Clan is people like me. I don't remember how they find us, when or where, it feels like I've been with them since I was born." No matter how far back in his memory he'd trawled through that long night, he couldn't find anything before the Clan. He remembered frightened boys like himself joining the group for training at about five years old, but they'd been with Clan teachers even before then. "There are maybe twenty of us right now; we live together, we're brothers."

"And what is it you brothers do?" Sinter asked the question in a slightly imperious tone, as if she expected Saker to respond that they played cowboys, or swapped football cards. She already knew it was going to be something more sinister.

"We're trained. Every single day we learn things, we study and we work, really hard." His memories of the training had turned out to be particularly lucid. He saw himself with the others, rising while it was still dark for yoga, meditation and breathing training. Then through the day there'd be endless sparring in every conceivable martial art, with and without weapons. They'd sit around in a circle as the teachers took them through everything from learning how to snatch someone's wallet without them noticing, to studying which plants you could eat or use as medicines or poisons. He'd learned which trees made the best bows and arrows and how to make a fire by exhaustively grinding hard wood into soft. It hadn't seemed like a hardship, in fact he'd enjoyed the competition and feeling his physical potential growing day by day. But then things had changed. Some of his companions had started going away, sometimes for months on end. Some had come back hurt, wounded, or traumatised from things they weren't allowed to speak of. Some had never come back at all.

"We're hired out. All over the world. Sometimes we just take things, pretend to be someone else, or get into people's houses, maybe go into someone's office at night when no one's there and pick up information." He paused now, wondering how far he should go. "And sometimes we hurt people."

6

Wolf wanted to hurt someone. This job should have been easy, but one of his own pack had thrown a spanner into the works, and now he was facing the wrath of the client. Wolf didn't like being admonished by anyone, let alone a short, dumpy, out-of-breath middle-aged man, like the one he found himself being brow-beaten by now.

"This is simply ridiculous, you are supposed to be good . . ." the white-suited man berated him. "No, you're supposed to be the best! Aren't you trained for years before you're allowed to take on a job like this? Do you have any idea how powerful our client is? Do you have any idea what he'll do to me if we don't deliver his tigers? And I can promise you this, Wolf, if I get it in the neck, I'll make damn sure that you get it even worse."

"So you're not the actual client?" Wolf brooded. "You never told us that!"

"What the hell does that matter?" snapped the man. "You've been hired to do a job, five tigers by the end of the month; triple the money if they're alive. So far we have one dead tiger, a badly injured security guard, and one of your Clan apparently on the run. It's a mess, and you'd better sort it out."

"Don't worry, we have a welcoming committee waiting for him when his train arrives," Wolf replied confidently.

"And how is that going to work?" asked the man. "You're going to pounce on him in a public train station? I don't know how much time you've spent in India, boy, but there is nowhere busier on earth. Why not just take out a front-page advert in the Delhi *Times* saying 'Young Assassins loose in Assam'?"

"We're not assassins," Wolf countered, but in a voice that showed he wasn't entirely convinced himself.

"You may have to rethink that, if you can't capture your runaway any other way. I want him back or dead, and I want those tigers in my possession by the end of the week. If not, I'll let the client know exactly who is to blame."

Wolf shifted from foot to foot, eyes downcast. "There is one other problem," he said. "Saker has taken a hostage. She's the daughter of the Assam Bindi tea plantation's owner".

Wolf expected another lambasting, but his news was met with silence. He glanced up. The man was staring at him with wide eyes.

"But don't worry," Wolf continued. "We'll make sure

she disappears quietly too; there will be no comebacks."

"Is there any other way you can make a disaster out of something simple?" White Suit replied. "You will do your job as you should have done before, and you will NOT harm any civilians. Do you hear me?"

Wolf nodded. He understood. He had better get word to the Clan members who'd gone ahead to the train station.

Sinter stared at a gap in the floorboards. She could see the tracks rittle-rattling beneath, like the rungs of a ladder zipping past during an interminable fall. She could only distract herself for so long, before the enormity of what she'd just heard clattered into her brain again. This boy in front of her was a killer. Trained from birth to steal and murder, and she was his captive. Yet he hadn't hurt her. In fact he'd rescued her from the attack dogs even though she was no longer of any real use to him. And now she sensed a vulnerability about Saker too. He was just like his falcon namesake, seeing life at a totally different speed to those around him. When enthralled in the hunt with senses blazing, he had a focus, an ease and alertness that was frightening. As long as the adrenalin raced, he was in his element, but as soon as life slowed to a normal pace he didn't know what to do with himself. Here in the train carriage, trying to hold a conversation with a girl of his own age he'd become awkward, restless, utterly out of place. Suddenly he seemed like the child he really was, lost in thoughts, a million miles away.

Saker thought back to his days with the Clan in their forest home. The Clan lands were in Eastern Europe, in the last great ancient forests on the continent. These wild dark woodlands were alive with stories, and were filled with boar, bear, elk, lynx and even wolf. The Clan were constantly on the move, making camp for no more than a few nights before relocating. It was, for the most part, terrific fun. Who wouldn't relish the opportunity to have a life that was one big camping trip in the wild forest, being taught to track, to hunt, to fight? The teachers lived with the boys, and watched carefully for antipathy between them, which was soon quelled, so arguments and personality clashes were unheard of. They were like brothers, a family, a pack. Saker remembered how they were taught to observe the ways of the animals around them in order to become more adept in the ways of the forest.

One spring he'd followed a small viper emblazoned with a diamond pattern to see it hunt. He watched how it selected its ambush position with great care to match its own camouflage, and chose a spot alongside a game trail that a small vole would eventually travel down. The viper invested all its effort into ensuring that everything was right, then waited, in total silence, without a twitch of its muscles, utterly patient. It was three days before a vole passed within striking distance, and when the snake struck, it was lethal and perfect. When Saker hunted after that, he would observe that same care and consideration in his planning, with the knowledge that when he did strike, it must be perfect – there might only be one chance of success.

But as Saker had got older, he had inevitably started to ask questions. The teachers never addressed what the Clan did, what the purpose was of all their training. The boys were encouraged to be free spirits, always learning from the natural world around them, always improvising, yet never asking the big questions about who they actually were or what their training might finally lead to. Truth was, the tigress in the thicket had been the tipping point for Saker. The teachers taught that the Clan was everything, that the outside world was cruel and stupid. They were taught about the horrors of people forced to live in tiny boxes, surrounded by roaring machines and thick poisonous smoky air, far from the life-giving bounty of the mother forests. Most were miserable lab rats, so it was somehow fine to steal from them or harm them. However, when Saker had been to towns and cities on training exercises, although never comfortable, he had felt that the city had an excitement of its own, and that not all the people looked unhappy or trapped. Questioning was simply not allowed by the Clan, though – the boys had to follow the teachings of the Prophet or face the consequences.

"I'm hungry again," he said gruffly. "Have you got any more money?"

Sinter shook her head. "You stole it all last night."

"You ate too, what are you complaining about? What about your necklace?" He gestured to the locket Sinter wore. "That would get us a proper meal."

Sinter started and clasped the locket to her breast protectively, turning away from him as if protecting a suckling infant. "No. We'll starve before you take this."

Saker had leant forward to snatch the necklace. "It's just a jangly thing," he blurted out petulantly. "If you were in the woods it would shine and scare everything away, it's useless. And I'm starving."

He reached forward again, but Sinter forcefully pushed him away. Instinctively, Saker raised his fist to strike her, but she didn't flinch, and something in her defiant amber eyes made him hesitate. After a few interminable seconds, Saker could hold her stare no longer.

"It was my mother's," she said. "It's pretty much the only thing of hers I have. It's more precious to me than anything. You can hurt me all you want, but you're not having it."

He slumped back. Sinter saw that her victory was a significant one. Saker's whole posture had changed, overwhelmed by her dominance. She couldn't help but soften; he seemed so lost and confused. For some reason, she felt the need to explain.

"My mother died when I was very young. I barely remember her, just that she used to sit and comb my hair after I'd been playing in the plantations. She had long fingers, and always used to wear a light blue sari, like a peahen's eggshells." She paused and thought for a second. "That's all."

"Was she very beautiful?" asked Saker quietly.

"Yes, she was . . . actually, I don't know. I always think of her as beautiful, but I can't really remember her face at all. When I see her in my dreams, she always has someone else's face there; Aisha Rai, or . . ." she laughed self-consciously, the idea of putting a Bollywood heroine's face on her dead mother's body seemed such a babyish thing to do. "It's so sad that I don't remember."

"We never knew our mothers or fathers," Saker said. She detected sadness in his tone now. "Though some of the boys claimed to, we always knew they were lying. We used to talk about it sometimes at night. Most reckoned we'd been stolen when we were babies, some thought we'd been made in test tubes, like clones or something. And the teachers never told us anything – they taught us all the time, but they never told us who we were, why we were there. And now I don't even have them."

"My father wants to sell me as a bride to a fat doctor who must be thirty years older than me. I have no home any more. I'm like you."

"You're nothing like me," Saker mumbled. "You don't know what I've done."

Sinter felt her stomach leap into her throat. "What?" she said in a slightly sick voice, and then trying to steel herself, "did you kill someone?"

Saker's eyes were still examining the floorboards, then

he looked up to the mountains, slowly changing their perspective as the train rattled on.

"This is my first big job, I realise that now. We were brought here to India probably two weeks ago. We never met the client, Wolf told us what we had to do."

"Is he the one who's chasing you?"

"Yes. He was always special, stronger than any of us. They had him marked out to be Clan leader from about five years old."

Saker saw in his mind the group sitting in a semi-circle in front of Wolf. When he had said Wolf was stronger, he didn't mean physically – there was no doubt that Bear was bigger and could have outwrestled him, but Bear was kind of . . . well, kind of stupid. Wolf on the other hand was a natural alpha, and had taken control with an ease and confidence that no one ever questioned.

"Wolf told us that the job was to bring in tigers – five of them. The reward would be higher if we brought them back alive, and extra credit would be given to any Clan member who did anything to harm the park guards protecting the tigers."

"What? But that's insane!" Sinter was incensed. "You've spent your life surrounded by nature, being defined by nature, and then you go out to wreck it? Why didn't you all say 'no'?"

It didn't make any sense to Saker either. "I know. The others were just so excited. Maybe a bit frightened too. But it didn't seem right to me. Tigers are . . . special. No

Clan member was ever strong enough to be called 'Tiger', and as far as I know they never have been. I told Wolf I wasn't sure what we were doing was right, and that's when the teachers put the plaster on me. After that, everything was like a weird dream, I was running, hunting, but it's almost like it wasn't me – like I was watching someone else doing it."

"And then what happened? It's not easy to find a tiger in India any more."

"We knew what we were looking for. It was only a few days before we picked up the trail of our first tiger. I tracked it on my own, following the spoor, I could smell it on the air. And a kill – I found a sika deer that had been taken and half eaten, so I knew it was close by. And then I found it." Why was he telling her all this? It couldn't do any good. Except it felt with every word as if he was getting the whole thing straight in his head, clouds were clearing, sense was being made of chaos.

"And you realised you couldn't kill it?"

If it was possible for Saker to shrink into himself any more then he did, visibly squirming.. "Eventually. Unfortunately by then it was too late."

"You killed him?" Sinter was aghast. This was worse than anything he had confessed so far, the idea of slaughtering a tiger, one of the few tigers left in the world. It was the most miserable crime imaginable.

"It wasn't a he. It was a she. And she had cubs. That was what got me. Suddenly I saw these two defenceless tiny creatures, and I couldn't do it . . . I guess even the drugs they'd given me weren't enough, but I couldn't let her suffer any more either."

He shook his head, just as he had then, as if shaking off a nightmare. The image of the tigress and her cubs would be with him for ever. "That's when I ran, and . . . and, well, the rest you know."

"But the cubs," Sinter said, "what happened to the cubs?"

"The Clan will go back for the dead tiger. If they find the cubs they'll take them too." He added matter of factly, "If they don't find them they'll die."

"We have to go back and find them." But even as she said it, Sinter knew this was nonsense. The cubs' fate was sealed. Sealed by the murderer in front of her. All her rage released like the valve bursting on a pressure cooker, and she lashed out at Saker, slapping him about the head and the body.

"Murderer! Murderer! You're one of those vile poachers I can't even believe are real people! How could you?"

Saker reeled back, putting up his arms to fend off the attack. Eventually, her anger spent, she sat back, sobbing. Saker paused a second, and then continued.

"I know. I know this is the worst thing I've ever done, and now I want to put things right. I'm not sure how, but I will make things right. I'm out now, and I'm never going back. I'll keep running for the rest of my life if I have to, but I'm never going back to the Clan."

As he spoke these words, the train began to slow, with a nails-raking-down-the-blackboard squeal of brakes on metal wheels. Sinter threw off her sack blanket. She was finally about to be free.

M argay and Polecat stared nervously at the train as it approached the station. "This is way too public," Polecat said.

"I don't see how it could possibly get any worse," agreed Margay, his eyes taking in the scene with growing apprehension.

Like any train station in India, the platforms, pavements and even the rails themselves were cluttered with people. There were hawkers selling sweetmeats, pakoras, candy and bhajis. Babas and sardhus – Hindu holy men in saffron loincloths – shuffled around holding their hands open for offerings from the passing throng. There were travellers and tourists, businessmen and pilgrims, old and young, and, even more disturbing, several blue-uniformed policemen.

"What's the formation?" Polecat asked.

"Bear and Cottonmouth have taken up a position on

66

the other side of the tracks," replied Margay. "Just in case Saker tries to break for it and into town".

"What about Mako?"

"He's going to board the train as soon as it stops, pass through the carriages, and flush them out into the trap." Margay said. "Just like the teachers showed us."

"Piece of cake," said Polecat, "if there weren't half a million people trying to get onto this damn train."

The Clan were as prepared as they possibly could be, but everything about the situation seemed to be conspiring against them. Before the train had rasped to a halt, people jumped off and onto the platforms, and the hawkers were trying to barge their way on board to tout their wares, or pressing at the open windows to sell to the passengers who remained on board. Without a word, Polecat and Margay split, each taking up strategic positions at opposite ends of the grinding train. If their targets got off here, they'd have to pass them. Margay reached under his tunic and pulled out a long knife that'd been tucked into his waistband, hidden in the small of his back. He held the handle so that the blade lay flush against his forearm, invisible to all but the most perceptive of onlookers. Polecat's eyes flicked around endlessly, his sensitive hearing no use in this melee. Even on high physical alert this was a nightmare scenario; the pair could easily glide past hidden in the crowd.

As Sinter jumped down into the dust, Saker was left in two minds. He had no duty to her, and was sure she'd be OK. She'd find a phone, and her wealthy father would have her whisked away within a day or so. And wherever Saker was going, he certainly didn't want her tagging along. She had no training, she'd just be a handicap he could ill afford. But something was telling him he ought to go after her. Just to make sure she didn't go to a policeman or anything. Besides, where the hell else was he going to go? He made up his mind, dropped off the stockcar and followed her at a respectable distance. Sinter pushed past the sellers, beggars and passengers, and clambered onto the stone platform trying to make her feet travel with a sense of purpose and direction that she really didn't feel.

Sinter spotted Margay just seconds before he saw her. He had the same close-cropped haircut as Saker, the same cotton tunic and combat trousers, the same awful intent about his physicality . . . she knew instantly he had to be Clan. Margay would probably have let her wander past, but for her startled reaction to him: the way she stopped instinctively told him he had found his mark. With electric speed he leapt forward, barging a protesting mother and infant aside, and clasped Sinter's upper arm. His talon-like fingers gripped almost exactly into the finger-shaped bruises left behind from Saker's assault the previous day, and Sinter winced.

"Where is he?" Margay hissed.

"He jumped off the train," Sinter blurted out, "sometime in the night, I was sleeping."

"Lies!" Margay retorted. "He would never risk jumping off a moving train in the dark, he knows better than that."

He yanked her back towards where he knew Polecat was waiting.

"There's no reason to protect him. You WILL tell me where he is."

With that he produced his knife and almost pulled her off her feet. It seemed impossible that such a slight boy could have such ferocious power. She wrenched backwards, half tripping over a blind beggar propped against the station wall, sending his battered mug of rupee coins scattering across the paving. Margay baulked. This was attracting too much attention, people were starting to stare at the brazen boy dragging a protesting and pretty Indian girl against her wishes. The disturbing trade in people still flourishes through much of the Indian subcontinent, and this could soon start to look like a kidnapping.

"You are coming with me, girl," Margay snarled, "conscious or not, so stop kicking up and make it easy on yourself." But there was less confidence in his tone now. People were mumbling and pointing. A policeman down the platform blew his whistle and yelled "Stop" in Hindi.

This was her chance.

"Help!" yelled Sinter, "he's trying to take me away, help me!"

As Margay turned his head sideways to see where the

policeman was he took his attention off his hostage for a split second, and Sinter stamped her heel with all her might down on the top of Margay's foot, where the thin metatarsal bones are joined by delicate muscles. He yelped in pain and surprise, loosening his grip on her arm for a fraction of a second, long enough for Sinter to break free and make a dash towards the policeman. He was a dark-skinned Bengali in blue uniform, truncheon raised and whistle still pursed to his lips, pushing through the crowds to get to Sinter. The crowd parted, but suddenly the policeman was hit side-on in a massive rugby tackle, crunching him to the ground. Bear! The outsize boy had blindsided the policeman and as he hit the floor, Bear rolled up behind him and struck towards the side of his head, in an attempt to knock him unconscious. The policeman threw his arms up in a protective gesture, and Bear's blow fell uselessly on his forearm. The police-man retaliated with a blow from his truncheon, and suddenly the two were locked in a struggle. Sinter would have to fend for herself. Sensing Margay behind her, she looked around to see a street seller frying dosas in a pan full of boiling oil. Just as Margay sprang, she turned and kicked the pan at him, like a football. The searing fat executed a glorious golden arc and hit his face with a horrid sizzling sound. He screamed in agony, falling to his knees with his face in his hands. Sinter sprinted for the exit, pushing past jabbering strangers, desperate to escape this crazy place.

The way out was through a high red stone archway, with ticket windows at one side, and an impatient crowd brandishing tickets trying to get past the barriers and ticket inspector into the station. The inspectors were so overwhelmed that they weren't paying much attention to the tickets of those who were leaving, and Sinter merely pushed past them and onto the street beyond. It was a carbon copy of many medium-sized Northern Indian towns, thronged with people, sputtering vehicles, and Brahmin cows lazing in the middle of the road. Vast gaudy billboards advertised decades-old Bollywood movies, a huge sunglasses-wearing actor with tailored moustache and coiffed hair glowered down from one peeling poster. Another warned of the dangers of drink driving, with the message '*After whisky, driving risky*'. In front of her at the kerbside was a battered old truck, its back door missing and replaced with a flapping blue tarpaulin. As Sinter made to dash across the street in search of help, her right wrist was seized, twisted up behind her, and a mere press in the small of her back propelled her forward.

The most effective martial arts focus not on matching force with force and actively fighting your opponent, but taking them in the direction they are already going, using their own momentum against them. In the gentle ways of judo, jujitsu and aikido a small protagonist can get the better of a giant, simply by upsetting their balance. This simple helping hand found Sinter – with a slight gasp of surprise – pretty much sprinting towards the truck, and being easily tossed into the back of it. She landed in the dark on a soft furry surface. Instantly the motor revved into action and the truck pulled away. As she made to sit up, the same hand pushed her down onto the furry rug she had landed on, stifling her screams, its talon-like grip threatening to splinter the bones of her wrist.

Saker watched all this unfold from a careful distance. As soon as he saw Margay seize Sinter for the first time, he became a ghost among the throng. He came face to face with a Hindu woman carrying a basket of fruit covered in a shawl to keep off the flies. He caught her eye, then effected a simple quick flick of his head towards Margay and Sinter. The woman's eyes inevitably followed his gaze, and when she was distracted, he whipped the shawl from her basket, ducked to one side, and threw the shawl over his head. Next he slid a length of stick from the firewood bundle of a man who had momentarily turned his back to get a light for his cigarette. Instantly Saker transformed his posture, bent double at the waist, the firewood becoming a walking stick. His shuffling gait metamorphosed into that of an elderly beggar, his height now reduced sufficiently so that he no longer stood out above the crowd. Saker's mind snapped into status report mode: "Margay will not be alone. The Clan will form a horseshoe formation, blocking all available exits, then drive the prey towards the waiting ambush; like African wild dogs, or chimpanzees when hunting down monkeys. Optimum team members, four blockers, one driver, and one back-up member with an escape vehicle."

He saw Bear crossing the tracks easily enough; Bear had never really excelled at stealth, not surprising really, he was double the weight of any other Clan member. Saker's brain skipped three steps ahead, weighing up all the possible outcomes like a chess player. The Clan had run through these scenarios a thousand times in the forests they called home. Every strategy was tried and tested with Clan members taking turns as "the mark", "the driver", "the ambusher". Every few months they would be taken into a town or city, and they'd run through their drills among an unaware public. In the forests, a kill would be registered by leaping on the mark and giving them a good beating. "Nothing aids learning better than a few bruises," the teachers would say. In public however the mark would merely have a smear of paint wiped somewhere across their person. The exercises could be carried out twenty times in a day in front of policemen and shopkeepers without them being any the wiser. Anyone who returned to the camp without the coloured brand would be rewarded with mangoes or bananas; perhaps even be allowed to sit out an early morning run, or the agonising battering exercises they did every day to deaden the nerves in their fists, knees and shins, turning them into more effective weapons.

Saker's conclusion was simple: Sinter was compromised

and must be sacrificed. Her inevitable capture would provide a welcome diversion to aid his own escape. And yet . . . He watched as she employed her canny trick, breaking free of Margay's grasp, before covering him in boiling oil. Saker was impressed, she was clearly more capable of taking care of herself than he had assumed. Now every eye in the station was on the fighting policeman and Bear, and on Sinter as she fled for the exit. No one would cast a glance in the direction of the crippled beggar stumbling just metres behind her. He followed as she pushed, panicking, through the crowds. As they went through the red archway, Saker looked round in search of transport. Bicycles were chained to railings. *Too slow, too much time to unlock*. He saw the sputtering three-wheel taxis waiting for passengers. *Even slower, and too identifiable*, and then he saw the truck. It had to be the Clan's escape vehicle. His stomach lurched, and he dropped his eyes, willing his body to shrink into the background. As he made to turn away, a slender figure came up behind Sinter. It was Polecat. He'd been right on her heels, and easily propelled her into the back of the truck before leaping in after her. With a bang on the truck's roof Polecat signalled for it to pull into the traffic. Saker's brain went into overdrive. The team was split, they would take different paths and rendezvous at a set time and location. Margay and Bear were incapacitated. Other Clan members would get as far away from here as possible. It was the classic evasion technique of a pack of animals, or shoal of fish, to dart off in different directions when under attack. Any predator would be confused by too many options, not knowing which individual to single out and chase. In such situations every individual would often escape; the worst-case scenario was that one or two slower members would be sacrificed for the benefit of the majority, who could regroup in the security of numbers when it was safe to do so.

Saker had at least a few minutes to make up his mind. Every bit of his training was telling him to melt into the crowd and get as far away as possible. When the boys had been briefed on the mission, they had learnt the location of several safe houses and a pre-assigned equipment drop. If he could get there quickly enough, he could pick up one of his alternative identities and be on a different continent before the next day was out. But then where would he go, and what would he do? Try as he might, he couldn't shake the feeling that he had a responsibility, and it was in the battered truck heading off into the exhaust fume-clogged streets. Before his internal hard drive could kick in with logic, Saker had straightened up, thrown down his walking stick and leapt into the busy road. A chugging motorbike rider leant on his high-pitched horn as he bore down on Saker. He moved to one side like a matador evading a charging bull, but as the motorbike passed him, he snaked out a hand and grabbed the rider by the collar, whipping him off the back of the bike, which carried on, sliding along the tarmac. Saker ran forward, dragged the heavy bike upright and, revving the throttle, skidded the back wheel around and swung his leg over it and into the saddle.

"What am I doing?" he spat through gritted teeth, and sped off after the truck and its flapping blue tarpaulin.

8

Gradually the pressure on her back eased, and Sinter knelt up, angry tears stinging her cheeks. This was the second time she'd been kidnapped in as many days, and she was beginning to fear every second would bring more manhandling, bruises and nasty surprises. Suddenly she longed for her jasmine-scented bath, and the bright smiles of the tea pickers. Even the indifference of Papaji would be preferable to this insufferable adventure. As the tarpaulin flapped in the wind, streaks of light illuminated her new prison, a flickering vision like the projection of an old-fashioned cinema screen. Her captor squatted, eyes darting about in the darkness, yet she could tell he was following her every movement.

"So what do they call you, then?" she asked in a tone that was as close to insolence as she could muster. "Laughing chicken? Hedgehog? Moody halibut?"

The hyperactive shape in the darkness looked back at

her with a mixture of scorn and annoyance. "They don't 'call' me anything. My name is Polecat. You might have heard of it, it's a predator that feeds on prey many times its own size," he said, leaning slightly towards her with an air of menace. "It kills by biting through the spine. You'd be very silly to underestimate the Polecat."

"A big weasel, then? Famous for a terrible temper and smelling like damp carpet!" Sinter was pleased at her cleverness even at a time of such mortal danger. She was surprising even herself at her ability to keep her head in a crisis.

"Just keep talking like that, and you'll end up in the same situation as her," Polecat sneered, gesturing at the rug Sinter was lying on. With that, a breeze lifted the tarpaulin, lighting the interior of the truck. The misshapen rug was emblazoned in orange, black and white stripes, and had a familiar form, and a pungent odour. Sinter stifled a gasp of horror. She was lying on a dead tiger.

Sinter had never been to a zoo or on safari, and apart from the riverside prints this was the closest she'd ever been to the majestic beast that had danced in her dreams for so many years. Even in death it was more spectacular than she could have imagined. The vast jaws were swathed in an extravagant white beard, long whiskers sprouted from the upper lips and around the nose. Sinter knew these were linked to sensitive nerve endings that allowed the cat to experience anything close to it through a peculiarly well-developed sense of touch. It could even pick up the tiny changes in the air made by the sweep of a bird's wings or the kick of a flailing deer. Ignoring Polecat she took a massive paw – it would have covered a dinner plate – in her hand. It had horny leathery pads on the underside that would've left a print much the same as that image from so many years ago. As she held the paw, Sinter pressed down on the knuckle, and the sheathed claw sprang forth, as curved and sharp as a domestic cat's claw, but as long as her index finger. It was at once the most noble and most tragic sight she had ever seen. Sobbing gently, Sinter wanted to throw herself onto the beast and embrace her, to somehow hug the tigress back to life. There was no doubt it was a tigress: the nipples were swollen and large, extended to suckle her youngsters. And there, above the teats was a dark, matted dried patch of blood, the wound that Saker's arrow had rent in her side. Sinter felt her anger rising. She turned to Polecat and spat out her retort with a ferocity that would have equalled that of any big cat.

"You are nothing but a vile coward, you can't think for yourself, and you murder innocent and rare animals. You have nothing to be proud of, you are nothing."

The violence of her attack seemed to take Polecat by surprise.

"I didn't kill her," he stumbled.

"But that's what you're here for. Maybe you weren't skillful enough to kill one yourself, but you're taking her to the person who ordered her killed. You're even worse than Saker, at least he's worked out that that what he's doing is wrong."

Polecat looked confused. His eyes flicked around, avoiding Sinter's furious gaze.

"You murdered her, and by doing that you murdered her cubs. If the authorities find you, they'll put you in a cage, one that even a weasel like you couldn't wriggle out of."

Sinter's newfound confidence was building; she sensed that like Saker, Polecat might be all sinews and murderous intent, but he too was just a boy, and vulnerable – she just had to figure out how to exploit that vulnerability.

"The cubs aren't dead." Polecat replied.

"Maybe not now, but they won't be able to take care of themselves. And even if they could, a leopard or village dog would soon finish them off," Sinter snapped.

Polecat's gaze darted to a crate closest to the driver's cab. Sinter suddenly knew, and lunged forward, but Polecat was too quick for her and threw her to the floor. As soon as things got physical, he recovered his confidence and he was back in charge.

"The cubs don't concern you," he snapped, "all you should be worrying about is getting out of this alive. And at the moment I don't rate your chances very highly."

To begin with, Saker used the traffic as a screen to keep his motorbike within close range of the truck. The bike dwarfed him – it was an Indian-made Royal Enfield, which is shaped a bit like an old-fashioned Harley Davidson, and growls along contentedly, but is about as slow and sluggish as a modern motorbike can be. It was one of thousands on the streets, and Saker could keep a close eye on his target without ever risking being seen. However, as soon as the town limits were breached, the traffic thinned out until the truck and the motorbike were the only vehicles on the road. Clan members are always alert to the possibility of a tail, and Saker knew a single glance in the rear-view mirror and they would spot him instantly. There was no way he could trail behind the truck within visible range There was only really one main road, so he dropped back a mile or so, and hoped to goodness not to lose them. Saker had only had a day of training on motorised vehicles, and was really struggling to get the hang of the clutch and gear system, so pretty much stayed in second gear, the engine whining with the strain of uncomfortable over-revving.

As the Indian countryside flashed by, he began to feel a real sense of well-being with the wind in his face. He was free! Nobody was telling him what to do, or where to go. He was making it all up as he went along. The road was heading into the mountains and Tibet beyond. He had always wanted to go into the Himalayas. The teachers had told them loads about the mountains: how to survive up high where the air was thin; how to prevent altitude sickness; to avoid the fierce cold of nighttime by digging a snow cave, or burying yourself in powder snow; how to fashion makeshift crampons out of battered tin cans or barbed wire. He knew loads about surviving in the mountains, but he'd never been. He'd never even seen snow or ice. That was to come later. If he'd come back from this mission. The mountains were a blue smudge beginning to loom over the future, swirling and grumbling clouds huddling about their peaks.

Along the roadside people sat behind stalls selling oranges, bananas and betel nut – a plant that's chewed to give a mild narcotic effect and stains the mouth virulent red. There were aimlessly strolling moth-eaten dogs, and lazing cows, broken down tricycle taxis and cyclists teetering out of the way of thundering trucks and buses. Every now and then he'd pass a pilgrim, heading north carrying poles over one shoulder with gourds at either end. These gourds would be filled with water from the source of the Ganges river, Mother Ganga, which erupts from a glacier under one of the most beautiful peaks in the entire Himalayas. Some pilgrims would walk three thousand kilometres – the length of the country – to bathe at the source, which they believed would cleanse their family of seven generations of sin. Then having collected sacred water, they'd walk all the way back again to share their good fortune with their loved ones. Saker marvelled at the conviction of the Hindu faithful; to believe in something so completely that you could sacrifice years of your life in the pursuit of an idea. He on the other hand had been told what to believe since his first conscious moments. He had no idea what he thought about . . . well, about anything.

It was liberating, but terrifying at the same time.

He passed a sign, placed by the Indian army: *"Don't race don't rally, enjoy beauty of Valley."* Saker smiled to himself. There was no chance of anyone taking any notice of that. There was only one rule on Indian roads: *"Might is Right"*. A big lorry thundering along takes precedence over everything except a slightly bigger thundering lorry. Bicycles and cars had to head for the verge, or be driven clear off the road. Saker had already nearly come a cropper two or three times, and it certainly hadn't helped that he still hadn't got the motorbike out of second gear!

It was time to take stock. He had no money, and the grumble in his stomach was screaming out to be taken seriously. The petrol in the bike wouldn't last forever, and the engine would surely overheat if he couldn't figure out how to change gear. Ahead on the road was a slick of tough grains, spread over the tarmac. It was rice, laid out here in a thin layer so that passing lorries would drive over the top of it and crush the husk off the grain, performing for free a task that would otherwise have taken much labour. Saker pulled up, and swept a handful of rice into his hand. It was crunchy, gritty, dusty, and much of it still contained the husk, but he was starving. He knew it would swell in his stomach, and at least stop him feeling so hungry. He forced down another handful with his eyes clenched shut, and then looked around for anything else he could eat. He was no expert on the edible plants of the area, and was hoping for something obvious; perhaps some figs or bananas, but had no luck. However, nearby he happened upon a green-leaved plant with anonymous yellowish flowers that looked rather like familiar pea plants. Not wanting to risk poisoning from something unknown, he used the tests that he had been taught, grinding up the pods and rubbing them first on the soft skin of his inner forearm. If it had started to redden or itch, it would have to be discarded. When there was no reaction, he rubbed a little on his tongue and inner lip, and again waited for a reaction . . . nothing. Finally, he munched on some of the pods, then dug up some of the roots. They were a bit muddy and gritty eaten raw, but full of protein. After an hour or so with no tummy gurgles, he ate a little more, while checking out the lower branches of nearby bushes. Here he found several thumb-sized bush crickets, with huge great long antennae, rubbing their wings together to make a chirruping song. Saker knew that insects – unless they're poisonous (and poisonous bugs usually have bright warning colours) have more protein in their tissues than beef. He pulled off the wings, and crunched into them raw, munching through the plasticky exoskeleton, and feeling them burst in his mouth like raw eggs. They were horrible, but he was desperate. Saker could feel the strength returning to his body with the few precious calories he'd put in. It would have to do until he could find some proper food.

Next he experimented with clicking the foot pedals on the motorbike, and after a few wild-horse lurches and crazy donkey kicks, he eased the bike out from the side of the road, and managed to take it all the way up through the gears successfully. The food had quelled the dragons in his stomach, and given him new direction. The pursuit was back on.

9

Wolf had his face in his hands. In front of the other members of the Clan he would never have showed such weakness, but he was alone, and massaged his temples in the vain hope that it would help. This was his first mission in charge, he had been favoured by the teachers, but it was all going horribly wrong.

Cottonmouth had just been on the satellite phone from further north, with the news of the botched ambush at the train station. Margay was badly burned, and confined to a dingy backstreet hotel with wet towels over his face and eyes. Bear had been arrested after several policemen had come to the aid of their colleague. Mako was yet to return to the recce point, and Polecat seemed to have taken matters into his own hands, taking the escape vehicle with its mercenary driver, the tea plantation girl and the package, and heading north; presumably towards the client.

And Saker? Saker had somehow managed to slip through an ambush of five of the Clan's best, and could be absolutely anywhere. It was the worst disaster ever to hit the Clan, and it had happened on a mission *he* was supposed to be in control of. Wolf had no idea how the teachers would respond, but he knew it would be brutal.

He had to call the Prophet, and tell him what was happening. Wolf extended the aerial on the Sat phone, waited for it to acquire satellites, and tapped in the number he had committed to memory. A voice he knew well came on the phone, and the hackles on the back of his neck prickled with fear.

"This is the Prophet. Repeat affirmation code."

The voice had been slightly electronically altered, and sounded a little robotic, but to Wolf the rhythm of the words was unmistakable. Wolf had three possible replies, one of which said that all was OK, and that he was speaking without any fear of being overheard. The second response was for a similar situation, but when it was likely the call was being monitored, and the third was if he was actually under duress – perhaps he'd been taken by an enemy or the police. Wolf chose the first response.

"A wolf mother howls to call her young."

"So why are you calling us, Wolf? The strict instructions were that you should not be in contact until the job has been completed."

Wolf explained the situation, his heart all the time sinking into his boots. The electronic alteration on the voice he heard from the phone could not disguise its fury.

"If I am to understand you correctly, we have one Clan member incapacitated, one AWOL, one arrested and another acting on his own initiative? How have we managed to get to this stage? It is time you took control of this situation, Wolf, or we will have to relieve you of your position. Bear has always been a liability. If he cannot be rescued without risk, he must be neutralised."

Wolf's guts jumped at this.

"Polecat must be contacted and told to continue to rendezvous point C. You will proceed directly to Danir Air Force base where you will meet a helicopter. Pick up Polecat and the packages and proceed to final destination."

Wolf breathed a sigh of relief. Trying to catch up with the renegades overland would have been a losing battle.

The robotic voice hadn't finished. "And Saker must be found."

A sharp intake of breath now from Wolf.

"But how? He could be anywhere. He's gone rogue."

The voice cut him short. "He is predictable. He is Clan. He will not be *just* anywhere, he has nowhere to go. The Clan is all he knows. He will be seeking to rejoin the group. Find him, drug him, bring him in. If you feel this cannot be achieved . . ." The Prophet did not finish the sentence, but Wolf knew what he would have to do. "We will not accept any further excuses."

As the day faded into a glowing orange light, Saker saw the truck had pulled up at the side of the road by a shabby hotel. It seemed likely that Polecat had stopped for the night. Saker drove past without so much as a sideways glance, then parked the bike a few hundred metres further up the road. He crept back through the rice paddies and small copses of woodland, until he could look over the corrugated iron fence, and into the rooms of the hotel. Not surprisingly, Polecat had pulled the curtains closed, to prevent prying eyes looking inside, but the curtain material was not sufficient to totally obscure the interior. Saker could clearly make out Sinter sitting cross-legged on the floor with her hands tied behind her back. A black uniformed thug who Saker instantly recognised as a mercenary was also on the floor, engrossed in a game of cards. A machine gun lay alongside him. Polecat was pacing up and down talking on the satellite phone, about something Saker couldn't quite make out, but he noted that Polecat looked far from relaxed.

Saker needed a plan. He couldn't just rush into the room; the mercenary had a gun, and with Polecat there too, Saker didn't stand a chance. He thought back to his training. He remembered the Prophet taking one of their classes on tactics: "Divide and conquer," he had said. "If a group is strong together, you must fragment them, take them out one by one. This is the predator's way. A lion cannot target a whole herd of wildebeest, it must separate the weakest individual from the group in order to succeed."

It was sound advice. Somehow Saker had to get them apart, but how? He thought back to what he recalled of the Prophet, and shuddered as he did. He remembered a tall, lithe man, the stubbly growth on his head coming through grey-white. He had gunmetal blue eyes and always dressed in a light blue Yukata kimono with dark trousers, the uniform of Japanese samurai and Kendo swordfighters.

The Prophet had an authority about him that would quell chitter-chatter instantly. The members of the Clan would sit around him in cowed silence. The boys had often muttered about who he might be, where he had come from, and if it was he who had set up the Clan in the first place. It was wiser not to ask. Saker remembered the fate of one of the Clan. Ratel was a grouchy sort, with a confidence in his own abilities that was totally beyond his modest size. In this, he very much mirrored his namesake, Ratel being another name for the honey badger, a small mammal that is so ferocious that it is known to drive lions from their prey, and eat the world's most venomous snakes. Endlessly inquisitive, with a foul temper, and utterly stubborn . . . let's just say Ratel was very well named.

For many weeks, Ratel had been gossiping when the teachers weren't around to hear him, complaining about the endless work they were forced to do, asking the other Clan members what they knew about the hidden heartbeat of the Clan, asking why they couldn't have their own clothes, choices, futures like the boys they saw on the outside when they went out on training exercises. Other Clan members would look around nervously, dreading that one of the teachers would hear.

One day, Ratel took things out of the realms of chance. The Clan were in the forest clearing sitting among the dry leaves, listening to one of the teachers as he explained the finer points of filtering dirty water by running it through a pair of socks and chunks of charcoal to make it drinkable. Ratel suddenly interrupted.

"What I want to know, what we all want to know, is what are we doing here? Why am I sitting in a forest listening to you? Why do I have this tattoo? Why am I learning all this stuff, what good is it going to do me?"

There was a collective intake of breath from the other Clan members. No one had any idea what would happen next, as no one had ever challenged the teacher's authority before. The teacher sat quietly for a minute or two, then carried on talking as if nothing had happened. Ratel sat staring at the dust, muttering to himself, but his outburst was never addressed. Saker and the rest of the Clan breathed a sigh of relief that the drama seemed to have passed without any unpleasantness. But next morning, Ratel was gone. His hammock had been taken down, and his gear was missing. It was as if he had never existed. Nobody asked big questions again.

The wooded copse was not especially large, but somehow in here among the dappled light and the chirrup of the bush crickets, Saker felt a calm washing over him.

There was something of home here. There was so much that was sinister about the shady world of the Clan, but right now Saker needed a little of their wisdom to solve his problem. "Divide and conquer," the words of the Prophet; he had to take down the weaker element of the duo inside the hotel. Saker had no doubt that this was the thuggish mercenary. However, he was also the guy with the gun, and Saker had nothing to defend himself with, not even a penknife! He found himself relaying a status report. *To the front of the hotel is the road and open spaces, to the rear fields (full of cows), directly west some scrubby woodland with cover. A narrow trail runs into it. That's my strong position.*

He thought back to the viper, hunting in the forests of the Clan land. Its success was all about picking the right spot, planning absolutely perfectly, then when one opportunity arose, making sure it didn't miss. Saker walked every centimetre of the wooded copse before deciding on the perfect place for his trap to work. Perhaps twenty metres in, he went down on his hands and knees, and used a stick to scrape a trench in the ground. The earth was hard, and Saker found himself sweating with the effort. He had hoped to make the trench deeper, but got no further than elbow deep before the ground turned stony and digging was no longer practical. He covered the hole with some thin sticks, covered those with broad banana leaves, then covered those with a thin layer of sand from the path. The hole was far from invisible, but Saker was planning to use darkness as an extra weapon. He stripped the twigs and leaves off a springy sapling next to the hole, then went in search of some rattan. Rattan is a natural wonder, a long thin vine with evil hooked thorns that it uses to climb through the forest. It is so tough that it can be made into cane furniture, or superlative rope, which will rarely break, even under extreme force. Saker made a short length of rope from the rattan, and used it to create a mechanical advantage, tugging the sapling into place. It creaked in its unfamiliar position, wanting to spring back, but Saker restrained it with more rattan. Ideally he would have created a trigger system, but without any tools he couldn't. No, the trap would have to be set off manually. It was a flaw in his plan, but there was no option. He tugged another long single string of rattan from the shrubs. This time he didn't pull off the nasty thorns, but left them, and teased the strand out across the path at what he estimated would be about head height. Now all he had to do was pick his time.

Inside the hotel room Polecat was still talking on the satellite phone and the mercenary had tired of playing cards. He had been hired for this job by someone he'd never met. Only a few weeks before, he'd been protecting businessmen who liked the prestige of having a bodyguard, but realistically were never in a million years going to get attacked or kidnapped. He'd just followed them to the office, feeling important wearing his dark glasses and pretending to listen to his very visible earpiece, then sat around all day drinking coffee and scoffing Danish pastries while the clients had their boring meetings. The mercenary, whose name was Jiugen, hadn't seen any genuine action for a decade, since he'd left the armed forces, and was rather enjoying this laid-back lifestyle. He'd become a little overweight on too many pastries and not enough exercise, and was struggling in the Indian heat. This present job was about the worst he'd ever had. He was being bossed around by a bunch of boys who looked about fifteen years old, and he was not enjoying the lack of a routine, along with not really knowing what he was doing. He just wanted to pack it in and go home. No one had ever mentioned to him that he would have to have any part in kidnapping some young Indian girl; not that he had any problem with that, but he felt it added extra risk, and so he should have been being paid more. It's fair to say that Jiugen was in a very bad mood indeed.

"So what exactly is plan now?" he asked Polecat. "You get instructions from the big man, or we still make it up as we go, eh? This is bad. We should ditch her, it is more trouble. This is not what I am being paid for."

"What do you know, meathead?" Polecat snapped, then instantly regretted it. He didn't need to alienate the one person he had to rely on. "We've been told we have to take her to the rendezvous. It's wise to stick to the plan."

"The plan? There is plan? It sure doesn't look like plan

to me! It looks like you make it up as we go along. And I'm not being paid enough. You tell your Messiah this from me."

"He's called the Prophet," Polecat bit his tongue, forcing himself to stay calm, wanting to add, "and he'd crush you for talking like that."

Polecat surveyed the hotel room. It was lit by a bright light bulb without a shade. There was a single bed between the three of them. That would be OK though, Sinter would sleep on the floor, he would sleep in the bed, and the guard could stay awake and keep watch. The cracked plasterwork was painted sickly pink, with plasticky curtains and big spiders lurking in the corners of the room. The cracks in the plaster had smudges of dried black blood on them, a sure sign that bedbugs were hiding inside. These beaked insects would come out in the night, stab their mouthparts into whoever was sleeping there and drink their blood, then spill some of it as they squeezed back into their cracks at the end of the night. They would all wake up in the morning with train tracks of itchy bedbug bites running over their bodies. Jiugin suppressed a shudder.

"This is heap big mess. Everything is go bad, I'm don't want going to prison because of some weird kid's army!"

He took a flannel from his pocket and worriedly wiped the oily sweat from his forehead, and from the bulldog-like roll of flesh on the back his neck.

"You don't need to worry about that. Wolf will find us,

95

and we'll be taken to the rendezvous. Till then all you need to worry about is driving."

"So what we do now? There is no TV here, no fridge, nothing. I want go get something to eat, my stomach she is crying."

"No," Polecat said firmly, "Wolf says we're to keep a low profile. Get the hotel to bring us some food in here." After a pause he added, "And get something for her too," nodding in the direction of Sinter.

With Jiugin gone to talk to the hotel people about food, Polecat and Sinter were left alone.

"So what happens now?" Sinter asked defiantly. "The thug is right, you know. You're guilty of kidnapping, killing an endangered species, and illegal trade in wild animals. That would send you to prison for years. And prisons in Assam are not nice. One of the workers from the plantation went to prison. He was put in a cell with about a hundred other people, fifty degrees, no windows and no toilets. He didn't last a month." This had never happened, but Sinter was concocting it as she went along and was warming to the subject. "A wild animal like you would go mad in a prison like that, behind bars, caged."

"They'd have to catch me first," snarled Polecat, but he didn't believe his own defiant attitude. Truth was, the idea of a prison really did make him shiver. He wanted this smart-mouthed girl to keep her opinions to herself and let him get on with the job. The operation had started to go wrong under Wolf. If Polecat could rescue things,

96

maybe the teachers and the Prophet would look fondly on him. Perhaps he could end up being the Clan leader instead of Wolf. All he had to do was follow orders, and get Sinter and the package to the drop-off without further incident.

"You should let me feed the cubs," Sinter said. "They could die in that box, they'll overheat. Then you'll have nothing."

Polecat was about to snap at her again, but stopped himself. She was right. They really should do something with the cubs. They were a substantial investment, and he would gain much more kudos if they got them to the rendezvous alive. When Jiugin came in, Polecat sent him out to the truck, and he returned with the big wooden box, several holes drilled in the top of it. As soon as he put it down on the hotel room floor, Sinter ran over and knelt in front of it. Jiugin untied her hands, and without even waiting for the blood to return to her fingers, she pulled the lid back. There was a tangible waft of hot air, and the stench of dung from inside. There, lying panting and with eyes weeping, were the two cubs, too dehydrated and overheated to even mew as the light was let in. Sinter gasped in horror.

"They are much too hot, cats can't sweat like we do, they'll die if we don't cool them down."

She could see how sticky the cubs were as they'd been licking themselves with saliva to try to cool down.

"You, meathead," she barked at Jiugin. He raised his eyebrows at her insolence. "Go and soak some towels in cold water in the bathroom and bring them here. And you, weasel boy, turn the fan up as high as it will go, we have to cool them down or they'll be dead before it gets dark".

The massive mercenary looked at Polecat to see how he'd react to being ordered around by the hostage. When the boy did indeed get up and turn the fan on full blast, Jiugin followed his lead, and went and soaked all their towels in cold water. As soon as he returned, Sinter wrapped the two pathetic-looking animals in their towels. Then she moved them so the air from the fan was blowing over them, this would increase the evaporation and cool them down as quickly as was possible.

"Right, now they're going to need feeding." Sinter chewed her lip and thought. The cubs were no bigger than a domestic cat, and she estimated no more than a few months old. Tiger cubs are weaned at less than two months old, so would probably be being fed fresh meat in the wild. They would however not be strong enough to munch up big pieces of meat for themselves.

"You," she was talking to Jiugin again. "Go back to the kitchen. Get me some fresh meat, anything, chicken, goat, whatever. And chop it up into little pieces. Then some milk and some sugar, or honey or something."

They might not drink it, but she'd seen this quick fix energy hit do wonders for human children who were ill with things like diarrhoea. "And some rehydration salts."

"What do you think this is, WalMart?" the mercenary

sneered. "There is no pharmacy here, we miles from any place."

Sinter thought for a second. What had she used back on the plantation when people were sick and needed an energy boost?

"Get some fizzy drink, a cola or something. Shake it until all the bubbles have gone, then put in some salt."

It would have to do. If she couldn't get the cubs to take on something soon, they would never make it.

With the repulsive thug gone, Sinter took one of the cubs, wrapped in its soggy towel, into her arms as if it was a baby. She could just about feel its heartbeat pitter-pattering. It looked so vulnerable, she couldn't believe it could grow into one of the world's most dynamic predators. When the meat came, she tried offering it to the youngster, but he showed no interest at all. His eyes seemed to be closing, it was as if life was simply ebbing away from him. This couldn't happen, it simply couldn't! Sinter took the bottle of cola, poured in some table salt, then shook it and shook it to mix it up and get rid of some of the bubbles. Then she poured some of it into her palm, and offered it to the cub. At first there was no reaction, then he sniffed at it, almost in distaste. But finally, to Sinter's delight he stuck out his tongue and lapped at the sticky liquid. She gasped at the roughness of his tongue, it was as if it was made of heavy sandpaper! When it was an adult, the tiger would use this tongue to shear off hair from its prey, and even to rasp meat from bones. Now, though, the cub was using its remarkable tongue to lap life back into its body. Within a few minutes, the cub was drinking a saucer full of flat, salty cola, and then with some sugar energy zinging around its body, it even managed to take the meat from Sinter's fingers. She could practically see the life force flowing back into the little animal's muscles. Next she set to work on his little sister. She was even quicker to respond, and made short work of the cola and the meat.

They were starting to get restless, and battling to get free of their damp towel prisons, so Sinter unravelled them, and allowed them to totter free around the hotel room. They started to explore, nosing under the bed and snuffling around the human occupants of the room. Jiugin shrank from the nuzzling cubs as if they were diseased; he clearly wasn't an animal lover.

Now they were fed, there was a new problem to consider. Sinter could hear the male cub's tummy gurgling, and he started to mew insistently. Sinter remembered reading that young cubs in the wild are not always very good at going to the toilet by themselves, and that their mother has to lick them around their bottoms to stimulate their urge to go. Close as she felt to her charges at that moment, this was rather further than Sinter was prepared to go! Even so, she dampened her hands in bath water, and tried rubbing around the cub's behind. He quibbled a bit, and half-heartedly bit at her hand, but then relaxed, dropped his hindquarters and did a massive dribbly poo and gushed about half a litre of warm urine onto the floor. Sinter laughed with delight. Jiugin sneered in dismay and disgust. "Oh this is just great. Now I have to share room with two crazy kids, and baby animals doing toilet all over the carpet. This is worst job I ever done. I hope you clear this up now lady, I not go near this . . . I definitely not being paid enough."

10

etween three and four o'clock in the morning is the time when the human body is at its lowest ebb. It's the time when sleep is deepest, and when anyone on watch trying desperately to stay awake will be closest to slipping into the welcoming arms of unconsciousness. Saker had no watch, so he forced himself to stay awake all night long. Every few hours he would wander past the front of the hotel, and glance in to the reception to look at the clock, counting down to the time when he should make his move. He saw the mercenary come out twice to speak to the hotel workers, and saw them bring in food some time later, but did not return to look in the window of the hotel room, not wanting to risk being spotted. As the sun sank, the sky bled red over the fields, the cows wandered around munching the cud, dragonflies danced over small glistening ponds like tiny hyperactive pixies. The beautiful bouncing flecks of light looked magical, but Saker knew the dragonflies were ferocious predators, with superior flying skills and remarkable eyesight, experts at catching other insects on the wing. At the same time, swifts and swallows were coursing over the fields snatching the dragonflies as they hunted. It was another stark reminder to Saker to play to his strengths, to pick his time and place with total care, and always to be aware that any second, a hunter can become hunted.

Saker sat cross-legged and meditated to focus attention away from his hunger pangs. He imagined his breaths being drawn into his body, flooding into his lungs, followed the oxygen as it transmitted into the blood and out to his fingertips. Then he followed the breath back out again, and emptied his mind. He focused on letting his shoulders almost melt as the tension slipped away, and felt well-being flood through his body. Polecat and the thug did not know when or if danger might arrive, and would not be prepared. When things started to kick off, they would be disorientated. Preparation was the key. The hunger was growling in his stomach, but he couldn't risk giving away his position at this vital time, so resisted sneaking in and trying to steal something to eat. Food could wait. As dark fell, the swifts and dragonflies went to their roosts, and bats and owls took to the skies. The calls of frogs and crickets began a dusk jamboree that was deafening, yet extremely comforting to Saker. At 3 a.m., he crept round the back of the hotel to look into the little room where they were holding Sinter, but saw Polecat still awake standing guard. He was pacing up and down the room, twitchy, but alert. This didn't fit Saker's plan, so he decided to bide his time, hoping that they would switch shifts sometime soon. When he came back just after four his prediction had come good. Polecat was out cold in the dingy bed, and the pudgy mercenary was doing his shift, slumped in a plastic chair. His head bobbed as he struggled to stay awake. Saker had thought of many tactics to try and entice the mercenary out into the open, but decided that something simple would probably work best. Saker steeled himself, walked up and stood with his face close to the window, then tapped on the glass. Jiugin nodded awake and looked up to see the face of the boy he'd been tracking staring in to the room. His mouth dropped open in disbelief. Saker smiled and waved at him. The mercenary sprang up out of his chair as fast as he could, and grabbed his rifle, swinging it up to his shoulder. But before he could take aim, the shadow had disappeared from the window. Jiugin shook his head. Was this some crazy dream playing tricks on him? But then there was a noise from outside, their truck had just started up, and was revving loudly! This was madness! Jiugin ran for the door, and stampeded outside, too late to hear the warning shouted by Polecat as he woke up.

Jiugin ran out to the truck, taking a line down the barrel of his rifle at anything that might prove to be a target.

What was the boy doing here? Was he alone? The truck was still standing where he'd parked it, but the accelerator was throttling hard, and the headlights were on full beam. He ran round to the driver's side door and swung it open . . . nothing! The ignition had been smashed, and the vehicle hot-wired. A brick had been placed on the accelerator to make it rev, but it was not in gear. Jiugin swung around now in panic. In the dark, the headlights only threw light over a small distance. Anyone could have been waiting in the shadows. Suddenly, there was a rustle from nearby bushes, and a bird took off, disturbed by something running below its roosting perch. Jiugin could just make out a path leading into the bushes. Fumbling, he slipped his headtorch out of his pocket and put it on. He had Saker on the run! With the rifle pressed firmly into his shoulder, and his heart thumping, Jiugin sprinted down the sandy path, his own panting drowning any other sounds. Which meant he didn't hear Polecat shouting, "Stop! Stop, you idiot, it's a trap!"

The beam of his torch illuminated a green corridor through the copse: the narrow sandy floor had fresh footprints leading away from the hotel. He ran now, heart racing with the fear of what might lie off in the darkness. Just then, his head-torch was ripped off his head as if some spiky-fingered sprite had leant down from the treetops and grabbed it – the hooked strand of rattan had done its job well. Jiugin stumbled blindly in the darkness, straight onto the flimsy twigs that covered

Saker's pitfall trap. He plunged in up to his knees with a yelp of panic, then heard an alarming swooshing sound. From his hiding place in the bushes, Saker had released the tensioned sapling, and it sprang forward in an arc parallel to the ground, like a baseball player swinging his bat. With a thunk, it hit the big man full in the face, flicking back his head and setting his thick bulldog's neck wobbling. Jiugin was overwhelmed, blood flooding from his broken nose. He stumbled backwards, but his foot was trapped in the hole, so he crumpled flat onto the ground in a heap.

He sat up with his face in his hands . . . and in the half-light found himself looking straight down the barrel of his own rifle. It was clutched in the hands of the young, cropped haired boy, whose finger lingered over the trigger in a manner that showed familiarity with weapons. Somehow Jiugin knew that Saker would not hesitate to pull the trigger if he needed to. Slowly he took his hands from his bleeding nose, and lifted them in the air in the universal gesture of surrender.

Sinter woke with a start for the second time in two days, as first the thug and then Polecat rushed out of the room, leaving her on her own. Her kidnappers had retied her hands before she slept, but in front of her rather than behind her back, and she'd been quietly working at loosening the knots. Her wrists were red raw, but she was close to being free. This was her chance. She sat up, and started to tug at the main knot with her teeth, teasing out one of the loops that would enable her to get free. Before she could even make a start on it, Polecat dashed back into the room, looking frightened.

"He's here!"

"Who's here?" Sinter asked.

"Saker. He must have followed us all the way from the train station." Polecat practically spat the words.

Sinter's heart leapt. He'd trailed her all the way here? They'd been driving for hours. Surely he'd not come to take the cubs back? She felt the rage building in her again, but then softened. It didn't seem likely. In fact it seemed more probable that he'd come for her . . . but why? Then her heart leapt again, but this time not in a good way; she remembered that the thug had taken his rifle.

"Will he hurt him?" she asked, trying not to sound as if she cared.

"Will who hurt who?" Polecat asked. "If I had to guess, I'd reckon the meathead is probably on his knees begging for his life already."

"You're scared of him!" Sinter realised with glee. "You know Saker's stronger than you are and you're scared!"

Polecat looked at her, and she could see she was right.

"We'll see who's frightened," he responded, and taking his long knife from his belt, yanked Sinter to her knees, and pressed the point into her neck. "Make another noise, and it will be the worse for you."

With his other hand, Polecat picked up the Sat phone from the table, and pressed the redial button.

Outside in the bushes, Saker knew he was back on top. He had the weapon, there was still a little darkness left to hide in, and he had the element of surprise. Saker took Jiugin's belt off him, and used it to buckle his hands behind his back. A search of his pockets yielded the sweaty flannel, which Saker would soon tie over his mouth to keep him quiet. His feet he tied with a long strand of rattan, and left him trussed up on the ground, helpless.

"OK, I'm going to ask you some questions, and you will answer me honestly. Who is in the hotel?"

"The boy, Polecat. And the girl. They are both in hotel room."

"And what about staff?" Saker wanted to make sure all avenues were covered.

"Just the old man who works on reception. The kitchen people all go home early. No other people staying there, and no wonder, I'm telling you, this place is a dump."

"Entrances and exits? How do you get into the room?" Saker demanded.

"The front door leads to reception, then the right corridor runs to the room, number five. And there is window at back I guess, but you know this already."

Saker slid the flannel between the big man's teeth, and tied it in a knot behind his head, making it impossible for him to shout.

"I will be back for you in a few minutes."

The thug mumbled through the gag, it was impossible to make out what he was saying, but it might have been, "I'm definitely not being paid enough."

11

The helicopter whirred through the semi-darkness towards its destination, its searchlights casting fierce beams on the ground below. The pilot was nervous. He hated flying at night using his instruments rather than his eyes, and had no real idea of where he'd be able to land. In a country where refuelling stops could be hundreds of miles apart, this could prove really dangerous. He also didn't know what the mission was, having merely been given a set of co-ordinates by the eerie young man who was his only passenger. Wolf himself was pensive and silent in the passenger seat. He wasn't wild about helicopters, or flying in general. He knew that none of his reactions or training would be of any use to him if things went wrong. He was not in control, and that made him nervous. For the hundredth time he looked at his GPS, and saw they were closing in on their destination, with no more than twenty miles to go.

The last twenty-four hours had been the worst of Wolf's life. Now he had his chance to set things right. Mako had finally arrived at the rendezvous, and had gone to the police station where Bear was being held. Miraculously, Bear was suddenly and without explanation released without charge; someone somewhere had paid a substantial bribe, or called in some serious favours. As Bear was now considered compromised, Mako was taking him out of the country and back to the teachers, in disgrace. There were still some other loose ends: Wolf had sent Cottonmouth to collect Margay and get medical help. The Prophet had given details of a doctor who would ask no questions and accept payment in cash. Not for the first time, Wolf marvelled at how far the influence of the Clan went. Even more so when he was told to meet the helicopter at an Indian military airbase. The young boy with his Western features and muscular shoulders drew quizzical glances from the pilots and ground staff as he was escorted through the base, but his paperwork was obviously in order. He was being protected by someone very powerful indeed.

After an hour of flying over plains, grey urban sprawl and then paddy fields and hills, the intercom crackled, and the pilot's voice came into Wolf's headphones.

"There it is," he said. "It must be that building down there by the road. I can land right out in front, sir?"

Wolf looked down and his stomach lurched. He was definitely not good at this flying business. "OK, set her down as close to the building as you can, and don't switch off the rotors, just keep her running, we may need to make a quick exit."

"Roger that," the pilot responded. Personally he would rather have shut down and grabbed a cup of coffee nearby. It was almost light now, and it would be much safer to take off again when the sun was fully up. However, he had his orders. The kid was the boss, and his orders were to be obeyed.

As the whirlybird neared the ground, the trees nearby bent away from the force of the downdraft, and leaves and dust were blown skyward, driven by the maelstrom of the whirring blades. As soon as the first skid had touched ground, Wolf saw Polecat sprinting out of the hotel towards them with a big wooden box in his arms. As the sliding door rolled back, Polecat pretty much threw the box into the back of the machine. He had an air of absolute panic about him, "The package is in the back of the truck, over there. Go grab it, I'm going back inside for the girl, and MOVE!"

Wolf knew better than to chastise Polecat for barking orders at him; something was badly wrong. He unbuckled his seatbelt, leapt from the helicopter and ran to the back of the truck, pulling the blue tarpaulin aside and dragging out the cool corpse of the tigress. She was nearly as heavy as Wolf himself, but he dragged her along the ground, and stumbled back to the helicopter. If it had been a male tiger he would never have been able to manage it; a large male could have been four times his weight. As he bundled the dead animal in, the pilot turned around, and his mouth opened with horror.

"What the hell! That's a tiger? You can't bring a dead tiger in here! What is this?"

Wolf shouted him down. "You have your orders, follow them and no one will get hurt. You have to take me, and my package, to the destination. Ask no questions, do you understand me? Ask no questions!"

At that moment, there was a whizzing sound, and a CRACK! and the windshield of the helicopter splintered around a fist-sized impact hole.

"What was that?" yelled the pilot. Then another whizz and a hole burst near the first, spraying the pilot with shards of powdery glass. "Someone's shooting at us!"

Wolf snapped his head round towards the woody copse – that's where the shooter had to be.

"I'm getting out of here," the pilot yelled, and started the throttle up.

The rotors started to race, whipping up the dust and leaves again. Wolf pulled himself into the cockpit, and saw Polecat at the door of the hotel, faltering and turning back towards them. As the chopper left the ground, Polecat broke into a sprint, dashing for the helicopter. At the last moment, he threw himself at the skid, and wrapped himself around it as it took off. He'd made it, but without their hostage. A hundred metres off the deck, he levered himself up in through the open sliding door, and climbed into the back of the chopper. With some distance between themselves and the bullets, the three occupants of the helicopter sat back in their seats and breathed a deep sigh of relief. The pilot looked around him at the two boys and their illicit cargo.

"Would one of you two mind telling me what the hell is going on?"

12

Saker and Sinter sat and looked at each other for the first time in twenty-four hours, neither really sure what to say or do next.

"So you've come to my rescue, then?" Sinter finally asked.

"Well, I don't know about that." Saker had gone from cold-blooded assassin to bemused boy in the blink of Sinter's eyes.

"You could have showered first," Sinter said, wrinkling her nose at the odour of sweaty boy. Saker was rather indignant, and thought about being sulky, then they both broke into giggles, relieved that the jibe had cut through the tension a little bit.

"Polecat took the cubs," Sinter said, suddenly serious again.

"The cubs? They're alive?" Saker was surprised at how relieved that made him feel.

"Yes, no thanks to your friends. They were in a sweltering box – it's a miracle they survived. But now they are in the helicopter, and heading who knows where."

"Let's get the fat man inside, and see what we can find out," said Saker, and headed outside to drag Jiugin the mercenary back into the hotel room. With the oversized lump sitting in the plastic chair, Saker loosened the flannel from his mouth.

Sinter looked at Saker's hands. Clasped in between his fingers was a long thorn from an acacia tree, pressed into the big man's throat. Jiugin couldn't see what Saker was holding, all he could feel was the sharp prick on his skin.

"This is a hypodermic syringe," Saker told him, "filled with the toxin from the suicide tree; you may have heard of it. If you lie to me, or refuse to talk, I will pump this into your veins, you will suffer incredible pain, and you will go crazy within the hour." From the look of terror on his porcine features, Jiugin was obviously taken in by the bluff.

"So, tell us where they are going," Saker said.

"I don't know! They tell me nothing! I am just the driver, this Polecat he tell me 'drive here, go there, fetch this, take this girl,' and I'm not being paid for this. I tell you now, you let me go I go straight home to Estonia. This is worst job I ever have."

"But you must know where they're heading to?" Saker was incredulous. "Where did Polecat tell you to drive to?"

"He just tell me drive north is all. He tell me drive north, then he talking to peoples on the Sat phone."

With that, Jiugin nodded towards the table, and the Sat phone lying on top of it. Next to it was Polecat's small rucksack. Saker concealed the thorn in his palm and went over to the table. He picked up the phone, and pressed the button that looked up the last numbers dialled. The last two were both prefixed by numbers that showed they were also Satellite phones. Saker pressed a few numbers on the keypad and rang the operator.

"Hello, Operator, I have a problem and I need you to help me. My friend is on a climbing expedition in the Himalayas and has just called me from his Sat phone. He is in trouble, his friend has been caught in an avalanche, but he has lost signal on his phone. I need you to tell me where he is."

The voice came back from the operator, "I'm sorry sir, that information is classified, we cannot give out details like that over the line."

"Listen, lady," Saker was firm now, doing a very good job of acting distressed, "these people are going to die. They are buried under the snow, I don't have time to go through proper channels, I have to get the rescue services to them. Now I know you can use Doppler Shift technology to locate the position of a Satellite device. Please, I'm begging you, you would be saving someone's life." There was a pause at the end of the line.

"OK, sir, give me the number and I'll see what I can do."

Saker waited patiently for the operator to do her thing.

He'd been taught that satellite phone systems transmit their signal to certain satellites in orbit around the earth, beaming information up to the satellite then back down to earth, in this case to another Sat phone unit. They're great for military and expeditions, because you don't need to be anywhere near a mobile phone aerial, you just rely on several satellites being in the visible sky at any one time. Luckily for Saker, it's possible to trace the position of a phone that's making a call, by triangulating the received signals back from the active satellites.

"I'm sorry, sir," the voice replied eventually. "There is no signal from that phone at this present time. It could be out of signal, or battery, or maybe switched off."

Saker crumpled. That had been his best plan. "OK, well can you keep an eye on it, and if that unit comes back online, will you call me, please? This is genuinely a matter of life and death."

"I'll do that, sir. Remember that that information didn't come from me. And if we do find a location, it can be out by several kilometers." Saker hung up and decided to delve into Polecat's rucksack. There was an ordinary mobile phone, a change of clothes, a toothbrush (suddenly he realised how badly he wanted to brush his furry teeth!). But the next thing he found was probably the most important. It was Polecat's passport. He flicked straight to the photo page. Polecat's fake identity was Robert Brown, about as forgettable a name as it's possible to imagine. Saker now turned his attention to the photo, of Polecat staring impassively at the camera, wearing a pair of broad glasses. The Clan deliberately had their passport photos as smudged and out of focus as they could get away with, in order to make it more difficult for authorities to identify the bearer. But right now this was a real advantage for Saker. The cropped hair and young face gazing back at him from Polecat's passport didn't look dissimilar to his own. His nose was quite different; Polecat's was broader and more substantial than Saker's. However, if he could find some glasses like those Polecat was wearing in the photo, the illusion would be pretty good. It probably wouldn't face scrutiny at a big international airport's security, but at a small border post where they didn't see too many foreigners, Saker was confident this little document would work just fine. The next thing he found in the depths of the bag brought a real smile to his face. It was Polecat's wallet.

"So what happens now?" asked Sinter.

"Well I don't know about you," Saker replied, proffering handfuls of rupee bills, "but I'm going to go and find some breakfast!"

The hotel manager was fairly frantic after nearly having his building blown down by a dawn helicopter landing, but when Saker offered some of Polecat's money to pay for any damage he soon calmed down, and sent for some staff to bring a mighty breakfast to their room. Having not eaten much more than a few handfuls of bugs in two days, Saker was beside himself with hunger, and started devouring dosas and vegetable curry with obvious relish. Sinter looked on with disgust to begin with, as he smeared food down his chin, and belched and chomped with his mouth open, ignoring every single rule of eating etiquette. However, much as Sinter wanted to show some restraint and be a bit more ladylike, she was famished too, and soon started shovelling the food down with endless cups of hot tea.

Saker was like a wild creature, getting as much food into himself as quickly as possible, never knowing when he might be disturbed at his meal, or knowing when he might have a chance to eat again. Sinter could see he would not be indulging in any conversation until his stomach was full to bursting.

Next came plates of sliced mango and tiny bananas with little black seeds inside them. All the while, the mercenary sat glowering at the two of them, clearly pretty hungry himself but the gag containing his drooling. Saker just kept on stuffing and stuffing! Finally he sat back with a great sigh of contentment. No sooner had he done so, looking as if he would collapse into a deep sleep, than the Sat phone starting ringing. It was the operator, with a list of latitude and longtitude coordinates. She again repeated her warning that this could be out by several kilometers, and the plea that Saker kept it to himself that she had given him this privileged information.

"So what does that achieve?" Sinter asked him.

"Well, Polecat called this Sat phone not ten minutes before the helicopter landed. My guess is that it's Wolf's phone, and we now have fairly exact coordinates for where that phone is."

"So, we'll need to get a decent map, or get to the internet and Google Earth, then we can pinpoint where Wolf is and the cubs too," said Sinter.

Saker took a deep breath.

"Yes . . . I think *my* next move is to go for the cubs. I got them into this predicament, now it's my job to get them out of it. Plus, of course, I have a score to settle with the Clan."

Sinter looked long and hard at the boy in front of her with newfound respect.

"So what's our next move?" she persisted.

"Well, my next move is to head to the nearest town and find out where I'm going . . . and to put you on the first train heading home."

"You will not!" Sinter was surprised at her own vehemence. "You're not going on your own. I want to see the cubs safe, there's no way I'm letting you go alone."

"Listen, Sinter," it was the first time he'd used her name, it sounded foreign on his lips, "you've proved yourself and then some, but this is going to be dangerous, nasty even. Plus you have no papers. I don't know exactly where they are, but it's north of here, and over the border in China. You won't be able to cross."

Sinter hadn't thought of that. That would indeed be a spanner in the works. "But those aren't your papers," she retorted, "can't we just find someone who looks like me, and steal their papers?!"

Saker was about to snort that this was a ridiculous plan, but actually that was exactly what he would have done if he hadn't had Polecat's passport. He had to admit that she was smart. And he would attract much more attention travelling on his own.

"OK. Well then we need to get to somewhere where everyone is going to be carrying a passport."

"An airport?" Sinter ventured.

"Exactly."

"What are we going to do with him?" Sinter asked, nodding towards the beefy Estonian.

"We'll just leave him here; they'll come in to clean eventually. By then we'll be long gone, and besides, I think he'll be heading straight for home, not coming after us." Jiugin still couldn't respond, but gave them a look which said "you're darn right, I'm not staying another day in this Godforsaken country!"

Saker paid the hotel receptionist and took his leave asking only how far away the nearest big town was, and also for a length of garden hose. Sinter watched with interest as he put the hose into the petrol tank of Polecat's truck, and then put the other end into his mouth. He sucked several times until he could sense the petrol was close, trying not to gag on the heavy fumes as they rushed down the tube. Then he dropped the hose on the ground, with his thumb clasped over the end. Once he could feel the petrol was moving, he placed the hose into the petrol tank of the motorbike and they could hear the liquid gushing in.

"It's called siphoning," he explained. "If the end destination is lower, and the weight of the fluid dropping down here is enough, it drags more fluid behind it."

"So why are we taking the motorbike and not the truck?"

"Well . . . the truck is slower, and more conspicuous. And, well, I don't know how to drive it! I've only just figured out the motorbike!"

This was the first time he'd admitted to her that he couldn't do something. Sinter decided it was definitely a positive step in their relationship. As she'd be sitting on the back, she took Polecat's rucksack, loaded up with bananas and mangos so they didn't risk hunger again. There was just the question of what to do with the gun. It seemed crazy to relinquish it, but it would be difficult to hide. Eventually Saker wrapped the rifle in a length of old curtain, and threw it into the bins behind the hotel.

"We'd not be able to cross the border with it anyway," he said with more than a little reluctance.

As Saker got on the motorbike, Sinter swung her leg over the seat behind him, and hesitantly put her hands round his waist. Saker stiffened slightly. He was suddenly acutely aware that he'd never had a girl's arms around him before. It felt strangely comforting. They pulled away onto the empty road, feeling full of purpose. This time they weren't being chased, they were doing the chasing. It felt as if they were starting a grand adventure, until they considered the reality of it, which was both liberating and terrifying, knowing that they were heading into unknown territory, tracking a band of assassins who would be armed and prepared.

"So where are we heading to now, boss?" the pilot shouted into his microphone. The tone in which he said "boss" was laced with sarcasm. "You want me to fly into North Korea or Afghanistan? Perhaps we could go rhino hunting?"

Wolf and Polecat sat in uncomfortable silence, looking out of the windows. Around them the high Himalayas were starting to soar into menacing snow-capped summits. The peaks were near seven thousand metres high, so big that the chopper could not fly above them – the air would have been too thin to support the whirlybird, and the passengers would have had to be breathing oxygen just to survive. Instead they kept to the valleys, the mighty mountains looming over them like giant thunder gods.

"I can't keep heading north you know, this is already disputed Chinese territory we're over now."

To say the pilot sounded a little irate would be like saying mosquitos are quite irritating insects!

Wolf passed the pilot a piece of paper with northings and eastings written on it, the numbers denoting their position by latitude and longitude.

"Here are the co-ordinates we need to head to."

The pilot tapped the numbers into his GPS device on the dashboard, then looked at the results that popped up, double-checked, and spoke angrily. "This is nonsense. That location is in China. You know full well we don't have clearance to fly into Chinese airspace. Are you trying to get us shot down? I'm turning back!"

Wolf's response was emphatic. "No, you're not. This is our destination. You will find that it has been cleared – the Chinese will not bother us, I promise you. You can feel free to call back to base, but I give you my word we will not be bothered, just keep heading north."

The pilot looked at Wolf as if he was mad. He looked at his charts, but they didn't really offer any relief. He was many miles away from a potential fuel stop. If they tried to turn back now they could well end up running out of gas and crashing into the forests. It looked as if he had no choice but to press on, taking an Indian Air Force helicopter into unfriendly airspace without permission. All the while the mountains loomed about them, seeming to mock and challenge their progress, making the tiny whirring machine seem like a windborne gnat waiting to be swatted.

Minutes later, an angry Chinese voice came through on the radio. The Indian pilot didn't speak a word of

Cantonese, but he didn't have to, the message was clear. Words to the effect of, "Who are you, and what the hell do you think you're doing flying into disputed airspace without prior warning?"

All three passengers stiffened, half-expecting that at any second a surface-to-air missile would blow them to oblivion.

The pilot responded in as calm a manner as possible, "This is Indian airforce Alpha Lima eight four niner, requesting permission to proceed."

He flicked off the microphone, sweat beading visibly on his forehead and upper lip, and turned to Wolf.

"What am I going to tell them? We're in big trouble here, man! The Chinese aren't going to take kindly to us violating their territory. What have you got us into here?"

Wolf had been given assurance that they would be allowed to continue, but this was the first time he'd ever been in a helicopter, and right now he didn't feel any of the certainty he was trying his hardest to show.

"Just keep repeating our call sign, it'll be OK, I know it will."

The Chinese voice came back, this time even more fierce and abrupt. It couldn't have been any more threatening. Suddenly, from out of nowhere, two fighter jets drew alongside the helicopter, one on either side, no more than thirty metres from the sides of the machine, so close that they could actually see the pilots in their cockpits.

"J20s!" shrieked the Indian pilot. "This is not good,

this is NOT good! They can outrun us, shoot us down, we are in deep, deep trouble . . . you'd better start working your magic, boy, or we're history."

It was clear the pilot was near hysterical. The fighter jets alongside them were impossibly sleek and black, keeping pace with them like a greyhound jogging alongside its owner, capable at any second of racing off effortlessly into the distance. Or of doing something far more sinister. All of the Clan's bush lore and abilities counted for absolutely nothing here. Wolf had never felt so inconsequential and exposed in his entire life. He knew he had to get control somehow.

"This is flight Alpha Lima eight four niner." Wolf could feel his own voice wavering. "We need to speak to someone who knows English, we have been given permission to proceed. We are heading to Lang Chu citadel, we are guests of the Gong."

He had been told that Gong was the title for a nobleman. That was all the information he had to work with. There was silence on the radio, the two fighter jets hung ominously, their speed obviously so uncomfortably slow that they looked in danger of stalling and falling from the sky. Suddenly there was a voice over the intercom, this time in English, though thickly accented.

"This is control tower at the Chinese border. Are you aware that you intrude on disputed airspace? You have two minutes to turn back, and then we have no option but to shoot you down."

"We've been given permission!" Wolf almost shouted. "We're guests of the Gong, please, there must be some mistake."

He looked across at Polecat, who was sickly white, his eyes wide with fear. Without warning, one of the fighter jets throttled back, and dropped behind them.

"Oh my God," the pilot stuttered, "they're locking on to us, they're going to shoot us down, do something!"

"We have been given permission by the Prophet," Wolf yelled into the microphone. "We are the Clan, we are travelling to Lang Chu citadel, please desist!"

For several tense seconds, nothing happened. The planes hung in tight formation, stalking the helicopter like cruising black eagles, keeping pace effortlessly, choosing their moment to strike. Seconds lasted an eternity, as the vast peaks raged past them, and the three sleek machines twisted and turned through the valleys.

"Please repeat affirmation code." The accented English voice was back on the intercom.

Affirmation code? Wolf thought, his mind racing. But then he remembered his confirmation with the Prophet: "A wolf mother howls to call her young," he repeated.

Polecat and the pilot looked at him as if he was insane; they were about to be shot down, and he was talking nonsense. Again, there was silence from the intercom, the jets hung waiting for an excuse to blow them from the skies.

"Affirmation code accepted. You will be accompanied

to your destination. Do not deviate from course."

At this, one of the fighter jets banked away swiftly to the left and was gone. The other pulled alongside to escort them through the mountains. They had been granted a reprieve yet again. The Prophet's influence had saved them.

13

Guwahati City, located on the southern banks of the vast and holy Brahmaputra River, is the largest city of Assam. Perhaps twenty miles before Saker and Sinter reached the city centre, the chugging motorbike brought them onto Highway 37, and the relative serenity of their journey vanished in a cloud of exhaust fumes. All of a sudden thundering trucks hung with wreaths of blossoms and painted in gaudy colours seemed to be trying to force them off the road and into the stinking sewage-filled ditches alongside the thoroughfare. Other bikes and mopeds kicked up endless clouds of dust and honked incessantly with blaring squeaky horns, as they rocketed round the cow-drawn carts and flea-bitten donkeys. Guwahati City houses more than a million souls in a breakneck, crowded melee . . . the perfect place for a pair of young runaways to become instantly invisible. As so often, whenever Saker found himself entering a big metropolis, his tension and discomfort mounted. This was a place where the solace of the forest might as well be a million miles away. Sinter on the other hand was filled with excitement, enlivened by the baffling array of humanity, the possibilities and the opportunities.

Their first stop was at a pharmacy. Sinter bought dressings, hydrogen peroxide, lidocaine, a needle and thread, and a few sundries for an emergency first aid kit. Next they stopped at a market to buy new clothes; for Sinter because she felt dirty and smelly having not changed her clothes in three days, and for Saker jeans and a T-shirt so he might be able to mingle more convincingly with the locals. They tried three dingy hotels before they found one that was prepared to let them check in without showing their passports, and finally found a place with a twin room and its own bathroom, so they could get clean and start to plan their next move.

First Sinter insisted on seeing to the wound on Saker's head. It was several days old now, and starting to look rather angry and gooey. She swabbed it with the hydrogen peroxide. The edges of the wound started to fizz and Saker winced, as the chemical did its sterilising work.

"Don't be such a baby," she scolded him, working the peroxide into the cut as much as possible, picking out the dust and grit, killing off all the bacteria lurking in the wound. Now that it was clean, she could see that the wound was deeper than she'd first thought. Normally she wouldn't dream of suturing a wound this long after it had occurred, but as the alternative was a whacking great attention-grabbing bandage around Saker's head, she figured stitches was the only way.

"Right, I'm going to put two or three stitches in here, that should close the wound up nice and neatly."

"Have you ever done this before?" Saker was trying to sound as if he was teasing her, but she could hear the nervousness in his voice.

"Oh yes, lots and lots of times," Sinter replied confidently. She didn't add that she had practiced loads of times, but only on oranges, learning the technique by pushing the curved needle through the rind, and trying not to pierce into the fruit itself. This would be the first time she'd actually done it on a human, but she reckoned that admitting that would only make Saker more nervous. He might even refuse the treatment.

"OK then, I guess," he said reluctantly. But as she started filling a syringe with lidocaine he stopped her. "It's all right, I don't need any anaesthetic."

Sinter snorted at his bravado. "Don't be a ninny! It doesn't matter how tough you are, once you have a needle piercing into your skin you'll want all the pain-numbing you can get!"

Saker giggled at the term "ninny", it sounded like something out of a 1920s comic book. The truth was, he was really impressed by how Sinter took charge of the situation, and how confident she seemed. As she injected the lidocaine into his scalp, he winced again, but this time she didn't scold him. She was too busy focusing on getting her shaking hand to steady.

Five minutes later, she'd put three neat stitches into his head, beautifully pulling the wound together. Within a day or two it would be barely noticeable. Until then Saker would have to wear a baseball cap to cover it, which would have the bonus of helping to hide his face. Sinter looked at her handiwork with pride. It was a work of art. Even Saker was impressed.

"Wow, that's pretty good, Sinter! How often have you done that before?"

"Oh, hundreds of times," she replied, before admitting, "but only on soft fruit, you're my first live patient!"

Having showered in blissful cold water for what seemed like an eternity, changed into their new clothes and eaten their fill with bucket-loads of delicious North Indian food, they set out in search of an internet café. They didn't have to look far, as telecom exchanges with internet terminals seemed to be set up on every street corner.

It took a while to find computers that didn't seem to date back to the Middle Ages, but they finally found a place that fitted the bill. It was on the fifth storey of a crumbling building with wooden and bamboo scaffolding holding it together, and housed a big darkened room, filled with young Indian boys wearing headsets, playing online games with people from all over the world. Nobody even looked up as Saker and Sinter walked in and took their place in front of a terminal.

Saker sat down at the computer, but instantly realised it was not the model he'd been taught how to use, and that he didn't even know how to turn it on. Sinter sighed, ushered him out of the swivel chair and took her place in front of the monitor. Within minutes she had Google Earth up on the screen in front of them, and had tapped in the co-ordinates the operator had given them, which they hoped would locate Wolf's position. The central point registered on the screen, and the focus started to zoom down towards it, with the viewpoint of a skydiver dropping through the clouds towards earth. As it stabilised, and the picture began to gain definition, Saker took a sharp breath. The image showed towering snowcapped mountainsides, tainted by few human settlements or roads. The Himalayas cover nearly a tenth of the world's landmass, and are unimaginably vast and impenetrable. This place looked like some of the most impossible terrain on earth. The cursor was hovering over something indistinct. Sinter zoomed in a little further, and as the picture started to sharpen, it revealed a small town perched on a steeply slanting cliffside, and a name: "Lang Chu".

Sinter began the job of printing pages from the screens as hard copies they could take with them, while Saker zoomed back out from Lang Chu to get a better idea of the territory. It was as he had feared. The town was well over the border in Chinese-controlled Tibet. It would be a long and difficult journey, involving crossing at least one border, which would need a lot of luck and some serious attitude to pull off. Not only that, but while they were in India at least Sinter blended in. As soon as they crossed into Tibet they would both stand out like sore thumbs. Things were getting more and more challenging by the second. It was at least two hundred kilometres to the border, and once they were off the main highway and onto minor roads this would be a serious slog. The one positive thing was that by the look of the map, Lang Chu would be totally inaccessible to anything but foot and helicopter traffic for much of the year. In the winter months thick snow would have sealed the place off from the outside world. During the nonstop rains of the monsoon season, the dirt roads would become an impenetrable mud-bath. But now it was summer, and they would be able to get close enough on the meagre trails that led unbroken from Guwahati, and all the way from the border. It would take at least one hard day to get that far. But first of all they'd have to sort out some credentials for Sinter.

The international airport was about twenty kilometres from the city centre, and had a surprisingly modern and expansive terminal. The two of them sat at a coffee shop nursing cups of chai, and discussed their plan.

"Right, well the trick is to find someone who's come off an international flight, so will definitely have their passport with them," said Saker.

"Can't we just get someone who's checking in for a

flight heading overseas?" countered Sinter.

"Well, we could, but then they'll have to get their passport out just a few minutes later. They'll find it's missing and raise the alarm. If we're really lucky, we could get someone who's getting off a flight and heading home, they might not realise their passport's missing for a day or more, by which time we'll be in China."

"So we have to wait at arrivals for someone to come through who looks like me . . . which could take a while . . . then we just pick their pockets?" Sinter didn't sound convinced.

"They don't have to look exactly like you," Saker said, "just about your age, Indian, female and pretty . . ." he stopped dead, and started blushing like a bruised peach. "I mean, looking a bit like you in the face . . . you know . . ." he petered out in embarrassment.

Sinter resisted the temptation to tease him further. It had been quite a compliment, and she was pleased. She decided to save his squirms by changing the subject. "I guess if her hair's not like mine I could get it cut, little things I can change, right?"

"Yes, exactly," mumbled Saker, relieved. "I don't think it'll be as hard as you imagine. And when we've found a target, we use a classic diversion tactic."

"Which is?"

"Well, here's what I think we should do . . ." and Saker outlined an idea which relied on a lot of luck, but might just work.

At the international arrivals gate, Saker and Sinter both found themselves pieces of cardboard that had been discarded by taxi drivers, with the names of the passengers they were picking up written on them. As those people had already been picked up, there shouldn't be any danger of anyone coming up to them actually wanting a cab. They stood opposite each other behind the barriers, and watched the people coming through, pushing trolleys laden with baggage, the typical mix of terribly stressed-out travellers and elated returnees, already discombobulated by their journeys, and therefore vulnerable. They waited for three hours without a single girl walking through who was even close to Sinter in appearance.

Finally the doors opened, disgorging forty or fifty passengers all clad in Muslim dress, possibly returning from pilgrimage in the Middle East. Saker's eyes instantly plucked out someone from the crowd, and he fanned his face with his sign in the prearranged signal to attract Sinter's attention. Sinter instantly focused on Saker, and then on the girl he was indicating. Her first reaction was utter indignation; the girl he was looking at was shorter than she was, yet a good deal . . . well . . . heavier. However, Saker clearly had his reasons, and she had to stick to the plan. Both Saker and Sinter dropped their signs and moved in on the girl, who was keeping close to two adults who must surely be her parents.

"Just be patient, just be patient," Saker muttered under his breath as Sinter moved in closer to her, but Sinter was playing the game step by careful step. She waited until – inevitably – a pushy taxi driver tried to take the target girl's bag off her and drag her towards a waiting cab. This was the only part of the plan they could one hundred per cent count on happening! The girl and her parents flatly refused the driver's advances, and continued towards the exit. As soon as the taxi driver had given up, Sinter made her move.

"Excuse me, excuse me, ma'am!" she called, moving up to the plump girl, with an air of considerable distress. "I'm terribly sorry to bother you, but I think that taxi driver may have stolen your wallet!"

The Muslim girl looked round worriedly, clutching her bag to herself as if it was all she owned in the world. Her parents turned at the same time, initially stern, but softening when they saw a seemingly innocent and well-dressed young girl talking to their daughter. First impressions are pretty much everything, Saker had told her, and he had been right. The Muslim girl looked at her parents questioningly.

"That man," Sinter continued, "the taxi driver, I think he may have picked your pocket!"

"Well, Asla?" the father ordered. "Check your bag, have you been robbed?"

Asla, clearly quite frightened of her father, hurriedly opened the side of her bag, and meekly pulled out her purse.

"No, Papaji, here it is."

"I'm so sorry," Sinter apologised, "I'm just so sure I

saw him take something from you . . ." And then, as if by way of an afterthought, "Perhaps your passport?"

"No, no," replied the father testily, "I have all of those," and with that he tapped his burgeoning back pocket, carelessly giving away the location of their passports. "Thank you, miss, but you are mistaken, now we are in a hurry, come on Asla."

Saker had been keeping his distance, and had skirted round in front of the family. As soon as they had turned away from her, Sinter caught his eye, tapped her back left pocket and nodded at the father, signposting to him exactly where the passports were. From there, it was all too easy. Saker followed them to the revolving doors that led out of the airport, and as they pushed through, made as if to go through at the same time as the father, bumping right into him from behind, then backing off with copious apologies at his own clumsiness. The snatch was so perfect that Sinter didn't even register it, and she had been watching out for it. As Saker strolled up to her with a serious face, she almost expected him to tell her he'd failed, but at the last minute he broke into a broad grin.

"We're on," he told her.

14

" **T**his place better be close, boys, this bird won't run forever – we're really low on fuel."

The pilot tapped the gauge in front of him nervously, as if the needle might suddenly leap out of the red.

"Not far now," said Wolf confidently. Below them, a raging whitewater river sliced down through the valley it had cut for itself. The lower slopes of the mountains were draped in lush pine forests, with Alpine meadows above them, ablaze with the colours of the mountain flowers that grew there. A herd of wild Himalayan blue sheep scattered startled on tumbly scree slopes as the noisy machine coursed down their normally peaceful valley. High above them the sharp and pointy peaks glowered like the fingers of some monstrous troll, snow and ice glinting and flashing in the mid-morning sun. The sharpness of Himalayan mountains is due to the fact that

140

they are geological newborns. As the landmass of the Indian subcontinent slammed into the Asian plate, the monumental force drove these mountains skywards. As they are so young, erosion has yet to wear them down to rounded stumps like the much older highlands of Scotland. It was truly breathtaking.

The helicopter with its sinister Black Hawk escort rounded a corner to reveal a new valley, and perched on the petticoats of a mighty mountain, an ancient walled city, designed many centuries previously to be protected from warring tribes. No sooner had they spotted this vision, than the pilot of the J20 gave them a little salute and peeled away, roaring along the valley at extraordinary speed. A voice came over the intercom.

"Alpha Lima eight four niner, you are cleared for landing. Head to the main square, we will clear you a landing site. Fuel is standing by."

"Thank God for that," said the pilot with evident relief, and banked the chopper towards Lang Chu.

As they drew closer, the toy houses became real. The city was surrounded by a vast stone wall. Some of the dwellings sprawled outside this protective girdle, the houses all built in ancient Chinese style, with white plaster walls topped with red-tiled multi-layered roofs that tilted upwards at the corners. Broad red and gilt wooden columns held the roofs aloft, and were adorned with intricate paintings and carvings. Towering above the town was a vast fortress of impossible grandeur, built into the rockface so it actually seemed to hang out over the valley. The buildings seemed to have a personality of their own, like a haughty emperor sitting on a throne. It was both beautiful and intimidating all at once. As the helicopter hovered over the stone ramparts, the pilot slowed to walking pace so they could locate a landing site. The main square was probably double the size of a football field, but was currently home to a bustling market. As they approached, Wolf could see armed men with pikes double their own height, dressed in ancient feudal armour, racing among the villagers, hurrying them out of the way. The market stallholders tripped over themselves to wheel their wooden carts from the centre of the square, clearing a space for the helicopter to land. The downdraft kicked up by the chopper's blades caused absolute chaos, blowing their wares, hats and chickens all over the square. At any other time Polecat would have thought it hilarious to see the villagers scattering like windblown dandelion seeds after squawking poultry, feathers flying everywhere, but he was too nervous to see the funny side. Wolf looked at the pilot who was biting his lip with impatience. This would be a very bad time to run out of fuel. Eventually, a suitable area was cleared, and he dropped a skid, then two, and finally with a huge sigh of pent-up relief powered down.

As they stepped out of the helicopter, Wolf was surprised to see the villagers calmly going back to their daily business. Despite the fact that Lang Chu looked like a citadel caught in a thousand-year-old time warp, the villagers had obviously seen helicopters many times before. The boys were greeted by a guard of important-looking soldiers, clad in impressive armour. Made from rhino leather, with shoulder plates that hung almost to the elbow, it was decorated with Chinese characters painted in gold and red lacquer, and had breastplates of bronze. The helmets cast deep shadow over the eyes of the wearer, making it very difficult to gauge their emotions.

"The Gong has been expecting you."

The speaker was surprisingly tall for a Chinese, towering over Wolf. Instead of a pike, he carried twin swords sheathed in an X shape across his back. Despite the heavy armour and his size, he was light on his feet and moved with cat-like nimbleness. Wolf knew a warrior when he saw one. He bowed deeply from the waist to show his respect.

"Many thanks, revered sir. We – who did not give you proper notice of our arrival – humbly ask that you find fuel for our vehicle, and food for our pilot, if this pleases you."

He didn't want to overdo the politeness, but the little he knew of Chinese customs meant he would rather be safe than sorry.

"With pleasure. My name is Zhijan. Now if you would kindly follow me, some food has been prepared for you. My men will bring the packages."

The pilot stayed behind to oversee the fuelling of the helicopter, while Polecat and Wolf followed the guard across the square towards the citadel. Broad steps led to a temple building without walls, cornered by vast jade-coloured columns supporting a grand roof. Vases filled with smouldering incense sticks sent clouds of sweet-smelling smoke into the air, monks in deep red robes swept dust from the dark-stained wooden floor. The boys couldn't fight the sensation that they had been transported back in time, it was almost impossible to believe that minutes before they'd been in a state-of-the-art helicopter.

Polecat had barely said a word since leaving India. He was totally overawed by the whole experience. If he could have faded into the scenery and made himself invisible he would have done. Wolf, on the other hand, drank in every morsel of the experience, as excited and impressed as if he'd been called to have tea with the Emperor himself. At the back of the temple, an archway led into another small square, and the entrance to the fortified citadel. It had stone walls five storeys high, yet without windows, and at its centre was a hulking wooden doorway with iron studs, guarded by two silent soldiers, their pikes poised, ready to impale anyone who dared enter. As they approached, the guards drew back their weapons and pushed the huge creaking doors aside. Polecat and Wolf exchanged bemused glances as they followed their warrior inside.

"Lang Chu was an ancient Tibetan stronghold," Zhijan began, with the tone of the world's grandest tour guide. "There was a monastery and town here for over a thousand

144

years. Even in modern times warring mountain tribes attacked regularly, trying to steal the women folk of the settlement, and to take any wealth the monastery might have. Once the Chinese invaded Tibet, the Gong took control of the monastery, and moved the monks out."

"Who is the Gong?" ventured Wolf.

"The Gong is the feudal warlord who has power over this whole region. He imposes the taxes, runs the military forces, regulates trade. He is a man of great importance and power. Throughout much of China this system broke down generations ago, but here in the high Himalayas we still make our own rules."

Wolf looked at the mighty battlements, the metre-thick walls, and the armoured soldiers. "But why is the city still so fortified now, sir? Surely if the feudal system is no longer active then you're not in any danger?"

Zhijan snorted, a small noise that told Wolf he could not be more wrong.

"These mountains are the main trade routes for all manner of . . . items . . . passing into and out of China." The way he said "items" made it clear that he was not talking about porcelain or food, but something illicit. Wolf decided not to push him any further on this. "This is a lawless place, and what the Gong does not fear from the vagabonds and bandits, he fears from those in power who would take what is rightly his. Any man with status has many enemies."

As he spoke, they entered a grand hall, with a staircase

which wound through the darkness, flaming torches in the walls lighting the way. At the top, they broke back out into burning sunshine. The boys caught their breath. They found themselves standing on a broad terrace, with a low wall around it. In front of them the whole valley with its mountain backdrop was laid out like the most magnificent painting in the world. The peaks were so dramatic, so unimaginably huge that the boys felt tiny, insignificant, in their shadow. Wolf found that after just climbing the few stairs he was painfully out of breath. Zhijan looked at him in what could have been either sympathy or disdain, it was impossible to tell beneath his helmet.

"You had best go easy for your first few days at this altitude. We are at four and a half thousand metres above sea level, as high as many of the tallest Alpine summits. There is less oxygen here; if you work too hard you will get altitude sickness very quickly. I will have some tea brought for you, but first let me tell the Gong of your arrival. I am sure he will be most pleased to see what you have brought for him."

Back in the hotel, Saker and Sinter were as good as invisible amongst kaftan-clad dreadlocked Western travellers. They sat face to face at a table covered with grotty linoleum, and shared rice and goat curry. Sinter was studying the photograph in the stolen passport with a look on her face that was half quizzical and half insulted. Eventually she

146

asked, "So how do you intend for me to put on this much weight in a day?"

"There are plenty of things we can do to change your appearance, don't worry about that. We need to get you a hijab. That'll help disguise your face a bit."

Sinter was a little disgruntled, but this was the best they had, so they'd just have to chance it.

"We're certainly going to need some luck," Saker admitted, glancing over at the photo in the passport.

Sinter paused contemplatively for a second, then made a suggestion. "We should do a puja!"

Saker raised an eyebrow. "A puja?"

"Like a blessing," Sinter said. "Hindus do it before any major undertaking, it helps to bring good fortune to your enterprise."

Saker looked at her hard. He had thought Sinter to be quite a rational no-nonsense kind of person, and this seemed out of character. However, he didn't want to offend her, so merely nodded, wondering what harm it could possibly do.

They left the city just after daybreak next morning, trying to get an early start on the chugging Royal Enfield. The backpack Sinter carried was now bulging with the things they thought they might need on the journey. Just at the north of the city they crossed the long wrought iron bridge that spanned the Brahmaputra River. On the bridge they dodged potholes that dropped straight down to the sacred waterway far beneath them, and the smoke-spewing ships and boats chugging their trade, oblivious to the near-death dramas going on above them. On the northern bank of the river, they found a small temple, and Sinter gave a few rupees to a monk clad in saffron robes to perform the puja for them. The two were led down to the riverside, where local people were washing their colourful clothes, and scrubbing themselves all over with soap.

The monk chanted some simple prayers and, using his thumb, placed a small mark of wet rice and red vermillion paste between Sinter's eyes. She then took the small tub of paste from the monk, and gently smeared a little on Saker's forehead.

"It's called a bindi, or a tilak when it's on a man," Sinter explained. "It's put there because this place is said to mark the seat of the soul. It will help with your concentration, and also helps to ward away demons and bad spirits." She turned her eyes away and said self-consciously, "If you believe that sort of thing."

Saker smiled. The broadly grinning monk then took handfuls of water and splashed it over their heads.

"And who's this guy?" asked Saker.

"He's a baba, or a sardhu, a Hindu holy man. This is part of his job, providing good fortune."

"I guess that's why he looks so happy," Saker said.

The baba nodded enthusiastically, and splashed more water on Saker's head. Then he handed them each a small boat of lotus leaves, with a candle in the middle, and blossoms from various flowers.

"The flowers symbolise impermanence," Sinter continued, "they are beautiful for a short time then die. The candle is enlightenment and the sense of sight."

"So what do we do with this?"

"Put it on the water, it will be taken by Brahmaputra across India and carry your dreams with it out across the lands and out to the sea."

The two of them placed their offerings on the water, and sat back to watch as the pretty little boats bobbed off on the ripples, and finally were caught in the flow of the mighty river, miraculously staying afloat, and with the candlelight still flickering. They sat in silence long after the offerings had disappeared, neither of them wanting to break the moment. Despite Saker's lack of belief or understanding, he felt more at peace, more complete at that one moment than he had felt in a long time.

"What did you wish for?" he finally asked Sinter, "or is that supposed to stay a secret?"

"No, no. I wished that our journey would be successful, and that we would find the cubs alive and well. That's all. What about you?"

"The same," he said. But that wasn't all he had wished for. He'd also wished that he didn't have to come face to face with Wolf, or the Prophet. He'd wished for strength and wisdom he really didn't feel. He'd also wished (though he wouldn't admit it) that somehow he could have his way of life back. That he could be back in the comfort of the forest, learning its secrets, training and following the beasts

149

of the woods. Somehow he knew that this could never happen. However, what he wished most fervently was that whatever lay ahead Sinter would not be hurt. He looked at her face as she stared at the river, which burned with the scarlet and gold colours of the early morning sun. She was his responsibility now. She was also the only person in the world he knew who didn't want to kill him.

After several hours on well-tarmacked routes, inevitably the road started to crumble. There was less and less evidence of human habitation, and they found themselves purring through many miles of bamboo forests and densely packed woodlands.

"Great for tigers!" Sinter shouted to Saker above the roar of the bike.

"And panda too I should imagine," he yelled back. Sunlight cut through the bamboo stems in stunning golden shafts, the wind gently shifting the massive plants from side to side. They had to bring the bike to a standstill shortly after, as a gargantuan black water buffalo stood impassively in the centre of the road. Its upwards curving horns were so broad, that perhaps eight girls Sinter's size could have sat side by side on them as if on a giant garden swing. As they came to a halt, Saker made to get off the bike to go and shoo it out of the road.

"No!" Sinter hissed to him urgently, "don't stop the engine, he might charge."

Saker turned round and looked at her quizzically. "Are you bonkers? I've seen these dopey critters all over the country, they wouldn't hurt a mosquito!"

"This is a *wild* water buffalo, they're a totally different story!"

She was right, this was one of the largest and heaviest members of the cow family, with the biggest horns, and a famously violent temper. The hulking bull turned to face them, chewing the cud, as if it were a cowboy chewing tobacco and about to spit. The beast shook its head and dropped its horns, scraping the ground with a hoof. Saker throttled the bike, and shot around behind the buffalo as it lumbered to face them, but it was too slow, they were already gone.

In the middle of the day, they stopped in one of the bamboo groves, and took some parcels of rice and vegetables wrapped in banana leaves from their rucksack, as well as bottles of water that had been rendered sickly warm by the harshly beating sun. The pair glugged it down as if it was chilled fresh lemonade, washing the dust from their parched throats. The simple packets of food tasted unnaturally good.

"Isn't it amazing how much better food tastes outside?" Sinter said.

"It's even better if you've found it yourself," Saker responded. "There is nothing on earth that tastes better than a fish you've caught yourself, cooked over a fire you've made from scratch. It's the best thing in the world."

Sinter thought this did sound particularly wonderful. "Would you teach me?" she asked.

"Of course. Maybe when we stop and make camp tonight. Well, if we've crossed the border by then."

They sat in silence for a while, chewing the last remnants of their meal.

"What are you going to do when this is all over, Saker?" Sinter ventured tentatively.

He stared straight ahead. For a minute she thought he hadn't heard her, or that he was simply ignoring her question. Then he spoke with a faltering voice. "That's the thing that's been scaring me the most." He picked at a stick in his hands, as if it was the most intricate and important job in the world. "I have to just keep thinking about Lang Chu and the cubs, because after them is . . . just nothing."

They both sat thinking for a good five minutes, before Saker started up again, in a quiet uncertain voice Sinter had not heard before. He sounded utterly lost.

"Every memory in my life is of the Clan. I know you won't believe it, but this task with the tigers, this was the first time it was bad. Otherwise it was the best life ever. We loved it. We lived in the forest, moving all the time, making camps, sometimes by a river where we'd find fish and mussels, sometimes we'd sleep way up in the forest canopy, and move around for days without ever coming down to the ground."

For a second he stopped talking and was transported

back, waking up in his high-slung hammock, looking over the side to a dizzying drop to the forest floor. The dawn chorus was almost deafening (even above the snores from Bear slumbering in the next hammock), like an orchestra reverberating about the trees. The Clan didn't use any safety ropes to move through the trees, even this high up. Like young monkeys, clouded leopards and ocelots they simply had to learn to judge their leaps well, and learn which tree boughs to trust and which to leave well alone as they might be rotten, or too frail to bear their weight. Any fall would mean death, so they moved with care, but soon they were as sprightly high up as any other primate. Even Bear, like his namesake, managed to be a competent climber, though he would never swing through the treetops with the grace of someone like Margay or Polecat.

"And I loved the teaching too," Saker continued. "Every day we learned something wonderful, something that made more sense of the forest, something that made us stronger and better prepared."

"It does sound fun," said Sinter, "but you have to remember what they were training you for."

"We never knew that. And nobody ever suggested for a second we'd be hurting anything – it doesn't make any sense. I mean we were taught to study the animals, to respect them for their abilities, to learn from them. We might take a rabbit or a deer for the pot, but never anything rare, and never for anything other than food."

"It sounds like you wish you were back there."

"I kind of do . . . I mean, I know I can never go back, but it was all just so . . . well, so simple. We were never afraid of anything, we were always encouraged to try things out. I had friends . . . more than friends, brothers around me every minute of every day. Now I don't have a single friend in the world."

"You have me," Sinter said seriously.

It might have been the corniest thing she had ever said, but she saw from the softening in Saker's face that she had said exactly the right thing. She fancied she even saw a tear glisten momentarily in the corner of his eye. But then he brushed it away as if it was a piece of tiresome grit, stood up abruptly and started packing the rucksack, trying to pretend the emotion had never happened. Sinter smiled to herself; he was such a boy!

"You know I'm on my own too now," she said matter of factly.

"No you're not, you can always go home to your fancy estate and your father."

"Not after this I can't. I've seen more of the world in the last three days than my father has allowed me to see in the rest of my life put together. It's been scary, and it's been . . . madness, but I can't go back now either. If I go back, it's to marriage to a man I don't even know, and a life as his servant."

Saker raised an eyebrow.

"Well, OK, not a servant, but not allowed to achieve what I want to achieve with my life. I've always kind of thought . . ." she paused. "Promise you won't laugh at me."

"Of course," he said, nodding.

"I've always thought I was meant to do something special with my life. That I was meant to make a difference. I can't do that as a wife who's not even allowed to speak out of turn in her own house. I didn't tell you, because I thought you might tell me not to, that it might give away our position or something, but when we were in Guwahati, I sent my father a letter. Just to let him know that I am alive and well, and not to worry about me. But that I am not coming home. Not ever."

Saker looked at her long and hard. She was full of surprises.

15

In the thin air, the solar glare beat remorselessly down, as if it was trying to dry out Wolf's eyeballs and tan his skin to leather. Wolf and Polecat stood in awe, too overwhelmed by the mountains to ponder their predicament. As the sun slipped behind a cloud, the temperature seemed to drop by about twenty degrees. From getting sunburnt in their shirt-sleeves, they suddenly shivered as the chill seemed to penetrate their bones.

"You wait till the sun actually goes down," a deep voice pronounced from behind them. "Up this high it's like going from the equator to the Arctic Circle the second the shadows hit."

They looked round to see a man of obvious stature walking towards them, his hands folded across his chest and into his capacious sleeves. The Gong had dead straight raven black hair that fell to his shoulders, and a pencil thin moustache that drooped down around his lips. He wore a simple embroidered white silk robe called a zhiju, tied round the waist with a purple sash. He was perhaps in his mid-forties, but despite a slight pot belly still walked with confidence, his head thrown back with an imperious air. The slight deference of posture the soldiers showed towards him left no doubt of his status.

"You have come far. Please, come inside, we have much to talk about."

He led the two boys through another doorway, into a dining room, with large open windows looking onto the valley. Wolf noted that he hadn't seen a single pane of glass in any of the buildings. At night these windows would be covered with hefty wooden shutters, and there was no sign of any electric lighting either. It must get pretty gloomy here at night-time, and in the winter when they surely couldn't have all these windows open. The Gong spoke as if he had read the boy's mind.

"We keep things here at Lang Chu as they have always been. When dignitaries visit from Beijing and Shanghai, they like to see it this way, it fits with their romantic vision of us, and means they see us as less of a threat . . . it lets us carry on doing things our way, if you know what I mean."

Wolf and Polecat nodded enthusiastically to show that they did indeed know, though neither of them had a clue what he was talking about.

"Of course it's not all like this," continued the Gong. "The deeper parts of the citadel are bored into the mountain itself, and there we have our own power system, run by hydro-electric."

"From the big river below?" asked Polecat.

"Exactly, free power once you have the turbines moving."

They sat down at the long table, and servants in simple dark tunics began to scamper around bringing food and drinks for the guests. First of all a tureen of rice was served, and ladles of steaming sticky rice were piled onto the boys plates. So far, so good. But then they placed in the centre of the table a platter bearing a tortoise. The poor creature had been cooked in its own shell. The Gong lifted the top of the shell off, revealing the meat and the innards inside, and started to serve himself. Polecat turned visibly green.

The Gong spoke, "I have to say, I am a little disappointed at the cargo you have brought. I have paid an awful lot of money to be brought a single dead tigress and two cubs."

Wolf stammered and started to explain. "We're really sorry that it has ended up this way. I'm sure the rest of the Clan have had more luck . . . we had an incident that threw us rather off track."

The Gong waved his explanations away.

"It is unfortunate, but there will always be small problems. I have ways of making this work to our advantage anyway. And your Prophet and I have a long-standing arrangement. Soon these troubles will be but a memory."

At this another course was delivered, greyish-brown

meat served in a thick chocolatey sauce. Polecat served himself enthusiastically.

"Is this goat? It looks delicious."

"Fruit bat," replied the Gong, "boiled in its own rendered down blood. It's very good you know; I have them brought in from Arunachal Pradesh."

Polecat looked at the plate in front of him and turned even greener. Wolf looked at the floor and silently implored him not to throw up.

"Do you perhaps have any other food?" asked Polecat. "I don't know, maybe boiled eggs?"

"Well we do have some 'boy' eggs," answered the Gong thoughtfully, "they're soaked for several days in young boys' urine."

And then, as if impressed at Polecat's daring, he continued, "I have to say I've always thought them a little disgusting. Or do you mean thousand-year-old eggs?"

"They're not really a thousand years old are they?" asked Wolf, incredulous.

"No, no," replied the Gong, "rarely more than four months or so, they should really change the name of them."

"I'm actually not all that hungry," Polecat said, his mouth cloyed with spit.

When the servants had gone, and Polecat had eaten all the plain rice he could manage to force down, he plucked up the courage to ask the question that had been on his mind.

"Please, sir, I wondered if I could ask, the tigers, what

do you want them for? I mean, what use to you is a dead tiger, or its cubs?"

Wolf wanted to hold his head in his hands. They were supposed to be treading carefully, taking care not to offend, and Polecat had just stampeded in like a bison in a pottery shop.

The Gong's response was not angry. In fact if anything, he sounded quite pleased with himself.

"China is the fastest growing economy in the world. We are the global superpower, no matter what the United States wants to think. Over one billion people now live in this country, and both here and throughout Asia, Chinese people are getting wealthier."

He paused, and sipped from the goblet of wine in front of him.

"When people get wealthy, they demand luxuries, and they don't care how they get them. For many Chinese people this means traditional herbal medicines, and they are willing to pay the earth for them. Not just tiger, but bear, snake, rhino. The rarer the animal, the higher the price it commands. About sixty per cent of Chinese people use these remedies . . . but tiger, tiger is where the real money is." The Gong laughed out loud. "These remedies don't work at all! That's not the point! If I wanted to cure people, I'd run a pharmaceutical company! What matters is what people believe, and what they are prepared to pay for. Every single part of the tiger is used. The bones are ground up into powder and put into tablets, ointments and syrups. One animal's bones make maybe four thousand US dollars. In Taiwan they sell a soup with tiger penis in it."

Polecat's eyes opened even wider.

"It is said to make men more virile, it sells for four hundred dollars a bowl. The eyes, the organs, not to mention the pelt, which for many rich people is the ultimate statement. Anybody with money can own a Ferrari, but a tiger skin rug? This is something special. Altogether, a single tiger might fetch one hundred thousand dollars. Now you see why this is such lucrative business for me."

Polecat was stammering now, he couldn't quite believe what he was hearing. "But there are so few tigers left," he said, "surely if you keep hunting them they'll become extinct?"

The Gong looked at him with an expression on his face that sent a chill up Polecat's spine. "My dear boy," he said, "I'm positively counting on it."

The Chinese border could not have been any more intimidating. The road twisted and turned up the bank of a steep-sided gorge, with a raging cataract thundering down the middle of it. Upwards and ever upwards the road wound, until eventually it reached a point where the river had to be crossed, and here was a towering stone bridge, perhaps a hundred metres above the flow. This was the border. On one side of the bridge were the customs for India, and on the other for China. Stern looking guards wearing khaki tunics with red collars and carrying AK-47 rifles were everywhere, and a long queue of trucks, bikes and people waited on either side of the border, looking as if they had been there for weeks. On the Indian side Saker and Sinter found a little teahouse, had what they hoped would be their last meal in India for a while, and discussed their plan of attack.

"So, if you have a plan for making me into this girl," – at this Sinter held up the stolen passport, turned to the page of the photo – "now's the time to tell me."

"OK," said Saker, opening the rucksack. "What I need you to do is eat everything on the menu. You might as well get started now, 'cos it'll take a while." Sinter opened her mouth, and was about to tell him what a ridiculous idea that was, when she realised he was joking. He laughed out loud. To Sinter, used to seeing him so serious, the noise almost sounded as if a ventriloquist had thrown the foreign sound into his mouth.

"Very funny," she said, "well, I have been thinking, and I've got some ideas. I guess first off, I can put this headscarf over my head, cover as much of my face as possible. Next, I'll use this kohl eye makeup, like she has around her eyes, and put some of it into my eyebrows to thicken them and make them darker. And this," she took a ball of cotton wool from the rucksack.

"This goes into the cheeks behind the teeth. Just enough to make my face a bit rounder. As long as I don't speak maybe nobody will notice."

She looked around at the rest of the props. "I guess I could roll some of these spare clothes up, and plump out my stomach a bit. Certainly quicker than eating myself fat!"

Saker had saved the best bit to last. A pair of brown-coloured contact lenses he'd bought in Gujawati. "Your eyes would certainly give you away otherwise".

"What's that?" she asked, pointing to a small white plastic tub on the tabletop.

"Ah!" said Saker with an air of mystery, "This is polymorph, you can buy it in any old hardware store – it's used in electronics and model-making and stuff. You put it in hot water, and it turns into soft plastic that you can mould into any shape you want." With that, he tapped the side of his nose with the signal that means, *and I'm keeping the rest to myself.*

As Sinter went into the bathroom to effect her transformation, Saker went into the gents, and poured the granules of polymorph into his mug of tea till it softened and coalesced into a soft lump like white plasticine. Placing Polecat's open passport onto the shelf in front of him under the mirror, he moulded the soft plastic over his nose, and teased it subtly into shape, while mentally working out their back-story. The officials might ask nearly anything of them, and they needed to have their stories straight. About twenty minutes later he was finished, and returned to the café. Minutes later Sinter re-emerged too. The metamorphosis was incredible. Such a simple job, but she looked the spitting image of the photo in the passport.

Her reaction to him was justifiably even more impressed. He had moulded a slightly hooked nose over his own, and with judicious application of makeup had totally blended it into his own face. A Hollywood prosthetics expert couldn't have done better. With a pair of glasses similar to the ones Polecat wore in the passport, nobody would ever look twice.

Over a last cup of tea they sat together and ran through their story repeatedly, then went outside, got on the motorbike, and slowly drove past the queues and up to the Indian passport control. On this side the checks were remarkably lenient. Security barely even looked at their documents, but leaving India was always going to be easy. As they drove across the bridge, the Chinese soldiers stared at them with what Sinter thought looked like suspicion. She was sitting side-saddle on the bike, with the headscarf drawn across her face in a manner she hoped looked modest. Her heart was thumping in her chest. What would happen if they were uncovered here? Would they be thrown into a Chinese jail? Nobody knew she was here, she could languish in the hellhole of a backcountry prison for the rest of her life. Or worse, China had the death penalty for many crimes, perhaps one of those was illegal immigration? Sinter had read in the newspapers about two Buddhist nuns recently shot in the back by Chinese soldiers as they tried to cross from China to Nepal. Certainly the military here had a reputation for shooting first and asking questions later.

As they pulled up to the guard post on the Chinese side of the bridge, an official stepped up and held out his hand. He made a demand in Chinese, which Saker assumed must mean "papers". Reaching into his rucksack, Saker took out the two passports, and handed them to the official. The official barked another demand in Chinese, Saker shook his head to show he didn't understand. They were starting to draw attention to themselves now, and other soldiers were looking on with interest, standing and slinging their rifles onto their shoulders, throwing cigarettes out of their mouths and onto the floor, spitting with relish. The official signed that they should get off the bike and follow him into a crumbling office that clung to the side of the bridge over the abyss.

Behind a desk, a fat official sat smoking cigarettes while simultaneously chop-sticking noodles into his mouth. His uniform hung open at the front, and goo ran down his chin and onto the stained white vest he wore underneath. Upon being given their passports, he threw down his chopsticks and wiped his face on his vest before barking some questions in Chinese. The pair stared at him blankly. He changed tack and tried English.

"Why you want go into China this way? Where is your permit? You cannot come through here."

Sinter's heart dropped. A permit? They hadn't thought of that.

Saker took up the cause, "Hello, sir," he said. "We are travellers looking to explore the fabulous Republic of

China. We have heard so many things about your nation, we want to see them for ourselves."

"Then you go Delhi, fly to Beijing. Don't come here with no permit and try sneaking into China. You have big trouble now, boy!"

Sinter fought the urge to intervene, but knew that etiquette would demand she as the girl should stay quiet.

Saker continued, "We're very sorry, sir, we meant no offence. We would merely like to pass through this beautiful part of the Himalayas."

The fat official sat back and let out a nasty laugh. "What is beautiful about it?" he sneered. "Rocks, snow, peasants, this place is the end of the world, why you want to come here?"

Saker drew in his breath. "Sir, we are pilgrims, and seek to visit your nine sacred mountains. Our journey has taken us through India, and now we seek to finish with the most important, the most beautiful: the peaks of the great nation of China. Without finishing our journey, seven generations of my family will not find rest in the Afterlife. Please, sir, grant a simple pilgrim this request."

Saker was taking a major gamble here, knowing that in reality the journey he was suggesting was impossible, and actually spanned the sacred peaks of several different religions. However, the fat man had the air of a discontented city man. He had probably been ditched at this outpost in the back end of nowhere for a petty misdemeanour. Saker was gambling that he knew nothing of sacred mountains, or anything much other than the contents of the next noodle bowl. The fat official rubbed the long hairs under his chin, and looked thoughtful.

"Can you explain to me," he finally demanded, putting both palms down on the desk, and leaning towards them, "you explain why a Muslim girl and a Western boy go on Taoist pilgrimage?"

They noticed the subtle change, as the two soldiers flanking the official dropped their rifles from their shoulders and shifted them into their hands. Sinter's heart plummeted.

"Sir, we understand that we are not conventional pilgrims. I am the product of a bankrupt culture, I grow sick of Western ways," Saker said calmly. "And my friend here, she comes with me because she is in my charge, and does as I say."

The Chinaman sat back and shook his head. He lifted the phone that sat on the desk in front of him.

"You have no permits, you tell me made-up story, you in big trouble, boy. You and your girlfriend too." With that he nodded to the two soldiers, who stepped forward obviously to take the pair into custody, while he started to dial on the phone.

"Wait!" Saker intervened. "Could you just let me have my passport for a second, I'm pretty sure there is a permit in there, I completely forgot about it."

He reached for the passport, and flicked through it, then passed it back to the official. The fat man took the document. He looked up sharply at Saker. He paused, obviously thinking hard about something, then picked up his border stamp, loudly thumped it down on a page in each passport, then passed them back across the desk.

"My mistake," the official said quietly, picking up his noodles. "Your documents are in order after all."

Then, waving them away, with a mouth full of noodles, he barked at his soldiers, who led them back outside to their motorbike. They revved up, expecting someone to stop them at any moment, to shout out, to draw a weapon, but it never happened. Perhaps a kilometre further up the gorge, Sinter just couldn't hold on any longer and practically burst.

"What did you do? We were finished, we were going to prison, how did you make him change his mind!"

"Well, I'm not just good at taking things *out* of pockets," Saker smirked, as he pulled the polymorph nose from his face, "I slipped a hundred dollars into the pages of my passport!"

"You *bribed* him?" Sinter shrieked. "You bribed a border official? You could have got us killed!"

"Well, we were already in trouble, what did we have to lose?"

They drove on well after sunset, aiming to put as much distance between them and the border as possible. After an hour, the road climbed out of the gorge and into a lush pine forest. Even with the rushing wind in her face, Sinter could smell the clean sharp scent of the pines. She held Saker tight around his waist as they bounced over the potholes in the road, proud of the way they had both managed to complete the first stage in such a difficult and dangerous task.

Not for the first time she pondered on how far she had come in a few short days. Had it only been last week that all she had to worry about was what dress to wear to dinner, or what made-up story to tell her father if she wanted to spend time with the workers? And here she was now, bribing armed border guards, a disguised fugitive on the run with an unpredictable boy, who she was warming to hour by hour.

Not long after the sun had disappeared, the dim headlight on the Royal Enfield gave insufficient warning of impending potholes, and after a couple of near misses, they decided to pull over and make camp. To be safe, they hauled the bike well off the road and covered it in branches, then made their way several hundred metres into the forest. Saker showed Sinter how to make a simple lean-to, finding branches with "Y" shaped junctions and burying them thirty centimetres or so deep. Then he placed a mid-pole between the Y, and stacked up sticks at an angle on one side of the shelter. Steadily he covered these with smaller and smaller sticks, and then with leaves to form a waterproof shelter. As they had no sleeping bags, they gathered great piles of dry leaves to cover themselves.

Next Saker set about making a fire. First he found a bracket fungus and crumbled it onto a flat stone, which would become the hearth.

"People have been using fungus as tinder for thousands of years," he told her. "Some dried barks like birch are really good too as they have lots of oil in them, but resins can be even better."

Sinter watched, fascinated, as he cut some rattan cord about a metre and a half long, and then a chunk of soft wood, which he placed on the stone and wedged under his foot. Next he threw the loop of rattan round the soft wood, and with an end of rattan in each hand, began to saw up and down, so the rattan cut into the soft wood. Saker had a look of fierce concentration on his face and the effort was evident, after several minutes the soft wood started to smoulder, and then to smoke, but he kept on sawing. Eventually he dropped to his knees and started to blow gently on the fungus. It glowed orange; an ember! Minutes later, he had added some crumbled bark, then successively larger kindling, and finally the larger logs that would provide the real fuel for the fire.

As they sat around the warming glow of their own fire, Sinter reached over and touched the tattoo on his calf.

"So what about this then?"

He flinched slightly at her touch.

"What's the story with that? Do they brand you like cattle?"

Saker visibly bristled. He felt a real connection, a pride

for the simple mark. It almost defined who he was. She could see he was offended.

"Sorry, I mean it's just a bit weird, that's all," she back-tracked, "I've never seen anything like it before."

"The tattoo . . ." Saker seemed to be struggling for the words, "it's nothing like a brand. It's kind of . . . well, let me start at the beginning."

Saker's mind was a swirl of images, he searched for the thread, for the beginning. In his memory a tableau was forming, of bare-chested boys crouching around a fire, flickering flames casting shadows across their faces. The boys were chanting an ancient rite, like a Masai war mantra. Some took a slightly different key, others pounded out the rhythm, bouncing the chant around like a shared secret.

"To begin with, we are nothing. Until . . . I don't know . . . maybe eight or nine years old, we have no name, it's just 'you eat this', or 'boy, get that'. But then every Clan member has to go through The Test."

In his mind's eye, he saw one of the boys brought out of the darkness. The other boys painted intricate markings on his face and chest, like the camouflaged rosettes of a jaguar, or armoured scales of a crocodile. Many hands span him around in front of the flames, breathing increasing to fever pitch. The boy almost fell into a trance with the spell of the chanting, the fear and the dancing flames.

"Every boy takes their turn. You run off into the night, alone, wearing only your trousers, no shoes, no shirt, no weapons or tools. They give you an hour's head start, then the Clan comes after you."

He remembered running, breath coming in terrified gulps, off into the night. His time had come at the full moon, and the forest was bathed in phantom white light. Every shadow held ghouls and vile traps. To begin with, the fire in his belly had kept him warm, but as soon as he started to tire and slow down, he felt chill with the midnight air. Sweat dried clammy on his flesh, and goosebumps sprang up all over his skin.

"You have to survive on your own, always running for the first twenty-four hours. If the Clan catch you before then, you get a good beating."

"A beating?" Sinter was appalled. It had sounded rather exciting up until that point.

Saker snorted. "Anybody who wants to be tough has to go through a little hardship. It's not as if they do any lasting damage."

The Test was all about proving yourself physically and mentally, a rite of passage from boy to young man. Saker had run without stopping for perhaps an hour before his adrenalin started to fade, and he realised that he needed to preserve his energy. From then on, he would run for ten minutes, walk for five. As long as he didn't go round in circles, his head start should be sufficient to keep him ahead of his pursuers. Navigation was difficult, as the dense woodland obscured the skies, the stars and the sun. However, he had been taught that in this woodland a certain golden lichen always grew on the southern side of stones where it enjoyed a mix of sunshine and rain, while moss grew on the northern side as it liked to stay moist in the shade. Provided he followed the direction indicated by this natural compass he would always lengthen the distance between himself and the Clan.

Sinter interrupted his thoughts. "It must have been so frightening, being all on your own in the forest like that. Weren't you scared of wolves and bears?"

"Of course!" Saker said, laughing. "I was nine years old, I didn't know anything! Now I know that they were the very last thing I needed to worry about. Wolves never attack humans unprovoked, and the bears are shy unless they have cubs. But when you're a kid, you think there's something that's going to eat you behind every tree!"

Sinter broke in again, "So even at that age, you knew how to find your own food, how to make a shelter and things?"

Saker shook his head. "We knew some things, but when you're running, there's no time to think about stopping and finding food. To set up a trap for rabbits or fish you need time, hours or even days in the same place. No, we were just running. I grabbed mouthfuls of water from crocks in tree trunks and puddles, but no food."

"You must have been starving!"

Saker recalled the hunger. A deep craving, growling in his stomach, and a dead lifelessness in his limbs that had him stumbling around like a zombie. The lack of sleep was even worse. By the falling of the second night, everything in the world had taken on a strange quality, almost as if he'd been hallucinating. It was like the world he was used to living in but seen through a slightly distorted pane of glass.

"The fear drove us on," he continued. "Fear of what they would do if they caught us. Also, if they found us within twenty-four hours, we would have to spend another year as a nothing, before we'd be allowed to try The Test again."

"How long did you manage to stay away from them for?" Sinter asked.

Saker smiled, with a mixture of pride and remembered horror. "It was nearly a week before they found me."

He had done better than anyone in that testing year, even Wolf. They had found Saker cowering inside a hollow tree trunk, rocking silently. He'd lost loads of weight, and was suffering from exposure and starvation. He shrank away from the boys who found him, as if terrified of what they would do, but The Clan had borne him back to camp on their shoulders like a fallen hero.

When they returned, the Prophet had personally taken a sharply carved piece of rabbit's rib bone, and a bowl of black vegetable dye. Dipping the bone into the ink, he repeatedly stabbed into the boy's calf, as the boy fought the overpowering urge to weep. A man doesn't cry, and this was an essential part of The Test. Even then, after all he'd been through, if he'd screamed, the Prophet would have laid down the bone with the work half done, and it would all have been wasted. Beneath the freely flowing blood on his lower leg, Saker saw the falcon's head take shape, hooked beak, wide open eye, simple yet unmistakable.

"The Prophet told me what my name would be. He said that I was swift, sharp and merciless. That I'd taken flight like a bird of prey, kept myself hidden from sight, shown keen senses and never given up from my task. That I would be Saker. After the falcon. It was the proudest moment of my life."

He remembered how every Clan boy had thought of little else in the months running up to The Test. What if they were to be christened Skunk, Mole, Wombat? The shame would be life-ending! They all wanted to be named after a scintillating predator: the white shark, the bushmaster, or the leopard. Saker had returned to the Clan bearing his name like a medal.

Not only did the Prophet choose the boy's name based on their natural abilities and personality, but they would thereafter be trained to follow the skills of their namesake, and inevitably boys would end up morphing into the character he gave them. After a few years, the tattoo was more than a name. It was their identity, their inner demon, their shadow and their soul.

"For people in the real world, a name is nothing much. Just a tag you answer to. For the Clan, the name sums up everything you are." Saker said this looking directly at Sinter, so she fully understood the import of what he was saying.

"I think I understand," she said. "I won't mock it again."

For a moment they sat immersed in their own worlds. Then she spoke. "If I were to be given a name . . . a tattoo I mean. What would it be?"

Saker looked at her for a few seconds, then spoke with certainty. "You are Tigress," he said. "Your bravery, your cunning, even your eyes . . . and whether you know it or not, even without the tattoo you have always been Tigress."

Sinter felt pride flooding through her. It was as if somehow Saker had spoken to everything in her, summed her up in a single word. She couldn't hide the smile on her face.

16

From behind the rusting iron bars of a cage no more than two paces across, the furious amber eyes of a male tiger stared Polecat in the face. Polecat had always been driven by scents, and the musty smell of the beast was intoxicating, drawing him to the bars. In a flash, the cat ripped back his lip in a snarl, ears flattened against his head, and swiped a massive paw through the bars. If he had cuffed Polecat, he would surely have killed him. Polecat leapt back in fright.

The Gong laughed out loud. "Even caged it is still a formidable animal, no?"

Polecat giggled nervously, but this time kept his distance.

After Polecat had finished what he could stomach of his meal, the Gong had led them both through the back of the citadel, and into the catacombs beyond. Once they had left the world of wood and marble behind, they saw a whole new side of Lang Chu. The caves had been hewn from the granite of the mountain, were lined with strip lighting, and had security cameras rather than soldiers watching the entrances. They had been taken deep into the guts of the mountain, and had eventually emerged into a large holding chamber, about half the size of a football field. The place was filled with cages full of animals. Wolf recognised Sulawesi macaques from Indonesia, blue macaws from Brazil, snakes coiled in woven baskets along with piles of elephant ivory and the pelts of various wild beasts. So this is what the guard had meant when he said these mountains were the trade routes for "items" undisclosed! But it was the cages that lined the centre of the room that caught his attention. There were eight of them, two empty, but the other six all contained fully grown tigers, hemmed into boxes that were barely big enough for them to turn around in. They rocked from side to side, and paced as much as they could, showing the classic signs of distress and boredom of a caged wild animal. It was a tragic sight. Polecat could hardly bear to ask the next question.

"So what are these tigers for?"

"These are the lucky ones," said the Gong, following Polecat's gaze. "These are my brood stock, my stallions and prize mares, as it were. These are going to be put into a captive breeding programme."

This sounded more promising. "So you're going to breed more tigers?" Wolf asked, "And then return them to the wild?"

"On the contrary," replied the Gong. "Right now there

are several thousand tigers left in the wild, and the price for a whole tiger can reach one hundred thousand dollars. Imagine how much money they will make when there are only one hundred left? The rarer they are, the more money they will command. Here in China we have probably hunted our tigers to extinction already . . ."

Wolf finished off the thought for him. "Once you have the same situation in India and Russia, each tiger will be even more valuable."

"But surely," argued Polecat, who just didn't get it, "surely they'll be harder to find, so it'll cost you more money to catch them?" And then suddenly, he looked around at the tigers in the cages and it clicked. "You're going to breed tigers specifically for their body parts."

"That is why these cubs you have brought me are so valuable," the Gong confirmed. "They will grow up to be fine breeding adults. Many people in the Chinese government have been fighting to try and make it legal to farm tigers for their body parts. Personally I hope this doesn't happen, as the price will stay far higher if I have less competition."

"And the tigers stay here, in this cave, with no light, and nowhere to run?" Polecat couldn't hide his shock.

"Is it so different to them being in a zoo or a private collection?" asked the Gong. "There are more tigers being kept as pets in America in people's houses and apartments than there are tigers left in the wild, and probably even more on tiger farms here in China. People keep tigers in

New York apartments, in backyard sheds . . .

"These tigers, they get meat, they don't have to fight or hunt, they are lucky. The natural world it is cruel, an old tiger will be torn apart by a young one, a male will kill any cubs that enter its territory . . . we save them from this cruel life."

He spoke with an air of finality that suggested the subject was closed for now. In all honesty, Wolf was just as sickened as Polecat, but he was rather more adept at playing the diplomacy game.

"It certainly is an ingenious plan," he said. Polecat stared at Wolf as if he was mad; surely he couldn't be buying into all this? At that moment, a klaxon sounded.

"Ah," said the Gong, "the Go-between has arrived. I'm sure he'd like to meet you both in person."

They made their way back up through the tunnels, Wolf and Polecat in silent contemplation. They would both be overjoyed to be out of this horrid place and back in the Clan lands, in their familiar forests, where the only animals were running free about them, beasts with their own majesty and destiny, not caged prisoners bound for the medicine cabinets of the ignorant. When they broke back out into the sunshine, they could hear the whine of an approaching helicopter, and again they witnessed the scattering of chickens and stallholders as the red machine dropped from the heavens and down to the square. It was quite a bizarre sight seeing two shiny new helicopters sitting side by side in the ancient citadel. All the more incongruous was the character who stepped out of the latest whirlybird. Clad in a white suit, a little rotund and wiping sweat from his neck and jowls with a handkerchief, he looked totally out of place here. The Gong went to greet the Go-between personally, and shook him warmly by the hand, as an honoured equal rather than as a guest or subordinate.

Sinter woke feeling a warm form breathing down the back of her neck, and stiffened, thinking perhaps a wolf or leopard had crept up behind her. Abruptly, the world came into focus, and she realised where she was. Beneath her duvet of dry leaves and under their hastily fashioned lean-to, the chilly forest dawn had given her a crick in her neck, and the firm ground below her bracken mattress had bruised her hips and shoulders like overripe fruit. The breathing form behind her was Saker, huddled close for comforting body warmth. She yawned deeply, and shivered with a chill that seemed to have penetrated her bones. It was tempting to just lie there in the foetal position, praying for heat to come from somewhere, but she knew she should force herself to get up, get her muscles moving and the fire blazing.

Throwing off the rug of leaves, she went over to the shifting white ash of last night's fire, fingers crossed that some life would still be there. Blowing on the charred remains of the logs, she was relieved to see red embers glow white hot with her breath. She added some tinder and kindling and within a few minutes was warming her hands round a joyous blaze. Saker roused himself and came to join her, nodding his good morning. He put an old tin can full of water into the sides of the coals in order to boil it up for tea.

"Right, well you said you fancied learning how to catch your own food," he announced. "How about you catch us our breakfast?"

Sinter groaned audibly. The temperature was still so chilly that her breath smoked and steamed like the fire, and all she wanted to do was gaze into its hypnotic depths. However, she had asked that he teach her some tricks, and perhaps the activity would warm her up.

They wandered through the forest, in the direction of the trickling noise of water. When the brook came into view, Saker took Sinter's arm, and stopped her going any further. "Fish have all-round vision, and are much more sensitive about stuff out of the water than you might think."

They dropped to their stomachs, and crawled right to the water's edge.

"Now, you need to think like a fish," he said in a hushed voice, not whispering, just talking very quietly. "They're making their way upriver, and wherever they find a sheltered place to rest where predators can't get at them they'll take it. So watch the riverbanks, look for an overhanging tree root, or a branch that kisses the water. They'll be there, near the bottom, just hanging out."

Painfully slowly, he rolled up his sleeves and slipped his arms into the water. In front of him was just such a place, where the gnarled roots of a tree had been undercut by the flow, forming a natural wooden roof over the stream. Saker stuck his arms in up to the elbow, then up to his shoulders, and ever so slowly walked his fingers along the bottom till his hands were groping underneath the branch. Sinter couldn't believe what he was doing, trying to catch a fish with his bare hands!

"It's called tickling, or noodling," he explained. "You look for the trace of the tail flicking the surface, then just tease the fish, tickle it under its belly."

He wore an expression of intense concentration, "After a minute or so, they fall into a trance, it's like they're hypnotised, and then . . ."

With a sudden, blindingly quick movement, Saker threw himself backwards, splashing water all over the bank and Sinter. She was about to shout at him, when she saw, splashing on the bank, a big fat trout, rainbow colours running down its flank, gasping hopelessly for air. He had really done it! Saker laughed out loud.

"Poachers love this method, because if they get caught by a game warden they're carrying no kit to incriminate them; no nets, no line, just a bit of knowledge and patience!"

They spent a good hour there at the streamside, Sinter trying out her newfound skill, with Saker advising her on the best spots to try. The first four or five times she went in too quickly, and either nothing was there by the time she got in place, or there would be a visible splash as the fish made its break for freedom. Eventually, she sensed a slimy shape, slumbering under an undercut rock. Ever so slowly, barely wanting to breathe, she started stroking it, as if it were a nervous kitten, caressing its belly with her fingertips. She expected it to panic and swim off, but it didn't, and after a minute or so, she knew she had to make her move. In one swift movement she grabbed it by the gills, and tossed the fish up onto the bank. A catfish! As long as her forearm, with bizarre tentacles from its bottom lip, her first ever fish! She squealed with delight, and Saker laughed along with her as he fought to grab hold of the bucking, slippery prize.

They made a trellis of green sticks over the top of the fire, and baked the fish over the coals, then picked off chunks of sweet flesh as they cooked. Saker was absolutely right, nothing tasted finer than a meal you had caught and cooked yourself. Once they had finished eating, Saker disappeared off for about an hour, and returned with handfuls of plants, which he stuffed into his rucksack. They stomped out the fire, covered as much of their tracks as possible, and then hopped back on the bike and set off, heading ever further north.

Though the track took them up steep hills and down again into valleys, the overall tendency was always upwards. There was no doubting that the air was feeling distinctly thinner. When they stopped to stretch their legs, even the mildest movements left them slightly breathless. The scenery too was changing. To begin with the roadsides were bordered with rice paddies, which were squeezed into the smallest gaps around lush green mountainsides. Hulking purple-hued mountains with snowy tops would occasionally peek from behind the green. Sometimes the rivers at the base of the valleys were bordered by broad, flat, grassy floodplains, showing the extent that the waters could cover in full force. Several hundred kilometers of rough roads later, and they passed through a small settlement that Sinter recalled from the Google maps. As they sat eating dumplings and rice in a filthy roadside eatery, they pored over the maps, and saw for the first time quite how far they had travelled.

"I really am a very long way from home," said Sinter with a hint of melancholy.

The estate was now more than a thousand kilometres away, and it was as if they had entered a whole new world. Increasingly, the purple mountains were the foreground rather than the distant background. They were no longer in the foothills of the Himalayas. They were completely swallowed, rendered insignificant by the mightiest mountain range on earth.

"We're very close," said Saker, pointing with his finger to a spot on the map. "We really can't stay on the road much longer." He bit his lip in concentration.

Sinter half asked, half stated, "I'm guessing that just

driving up to the front gate of Lang Chu wouldn't be a good idea?"

"I don't think so. I think at the very least we should approach through the forest from here." He traced his finger along the road, then through the green colour to the side of it. "Which should bring us down to the valley opposite the town. We can get a proper view of what we're dealing with from there."

There were a few jobs they needed to do before plunging into the abyss. Sinter took their old clothes off to find a washerwoman, with a special request for their treatment, while Saker went door-to-door trying to beg, borrow or steal a few last-minute essentials. As it was already near the end of the day, they decided to stay in the village for the night. At their present altitude, another night out would have been more than just uncomfortable; they might have frozen to death. Instead they clustered round a blazing stove in a smoky wooden shack, the walls blackened from the constant smouldering.

The Tibetan family who lived there had broad smiling faces, with narrowed eyes to keep out the ferocious high altitude sun, teeth gleaming white from faces tanned nut brown and taut like leather. The women had their jet-black hair tied back in bunches, the men wore theirs long and topped with red caps. They smiled easily and readily, and shared copious cups of spicy tea with their guests. Sinter thought them the most handsome people she had ever encountered. The tea though was not to her taste. It had cardamom and other spices in it, and then a great lump of greasy yak butter dropped in. It was heavy and pungent, and nothing like the delicate fresh infusion she was used to at home. For the first time she felt a pang of homesickness. For a second she was taken back to the humid swelter of the plantation, the gaily-dressed workers, the scents of jasmine and honeysuckle round the house, and the heavy smell in the air after the first monsoon rains. It couldn't be more different to the thin, clean odourless air at this altitude. Or to the choking smoky air here in the family's shack.

They laid their heads down on piles of rather itchy blankets in a corner of the room. The whole family was sleeping in here, including their young children, so the pair took care not to make any noise that would have woken them. They needn't have bothered, the others were snoring almost as soon as their heads were down.

"Saker," whispered Sinter, not wanting to wake him if he'd already slipped into sleep. He turned round to face her.

"What's up?"

"What do you think is going to happen tomorrow?" she asked.

Saker didn't answer immediately. "Are you scared?" he asked.

"No!" she responded, too quickly and indignantly.

"Well, you should be," he said. "I'm scared. Tomorrow we are going to try and break into a fortress that we know little or nothing about. It will be guarded. There will be members of the Clan there, probably armed soldiers. And if they find us . . ." he sighed and shrugged. "We are going to just try and walk in there, and walk out with an armful of tigers. What could possibly go wrong?! Even if we do succeed, we'll be in the middle of Chinese-controlled Tibet, with inadequate papers . . ."

"And an armful of tigers," finished Sinter.

"Exactly." He paused for a second, trying to figure how to phrase his next sentence. "I have to ask you this, Sinter. We cannot succeed. We are going to fail, and we may well be killed. I need to ask you to go home now. Go and turn yourself in, say you were kidnapped, go home before it's too late. I can't be responsible for your safety from here on in."

She turned her amber eyes on him with a directness he'd never felt before. Even in the darkness her stare was so intense he needed to look away.

"Are you saying you want me to go, or advising me to go?"

Saker's silence spoke volumes.

"Because whether you like it or not, you have not been responsible for my safety for a long time now. We are a team, a partnership. I watch your back and you watch mine." She searched her mind for a way of putting it that would make sense to him.

"Falcons may be solitary birds, and they may hunt on their own, but it's a lonely life, and they miss their kills more often than they succeed. But black eagles hunt as a pair, working together to confuse and distract their prey.

Alone they are strong, together they are stronger. On your own you have no chance. Together . . . if we work together the odds may be a little improved."

Saker nodded. He nibbled his lip earnestly, "I was kind of hoping you'd say that. Actually I didn't really want you to go."

"We make a pretty good team," Sinter whispered.

Saker looked into her transfixing eyes as if he just couldn't tear his gaze away.

"You know, when I was a little girl, I wanted to be a doctor," she said. "I wanted to make a difference, to make the world a better place. A few days ago that dream was taken from me by the person I trusted most. Now I have another chance to make a difference. You won't get rid of me that easily. Now get some sleep," she said, and rolled over, pulling her blankets tight around her.

17

Wolf and Polecat too were deep in night-time conversation, and the subject would have been of great interest to the runaways sleeping not too far away.

"This place is evil, Wolf." Polecat was almost in tears as he spoke. "I can't bear to see those tigers like that, in cages, it's just wrong, they should be running free, hunting deer." And again, "I can't bear it."

They were in two beds side by side, hewn out of crudely cut ironwood. The mattresses were deep and welcoming, the duvets smelled of lavender and pine. They should have been sleeping soundly as the dead, but were both wide-eyed and miles from sleep's embrace.

"I know it seems all wrong," Wolf countered, "but it's simple economics. Rich people will get what they want no matter what the cost. We can't be expected to change the world, Polecat."

"We don't have to change the world, Wolf, but we also don't have to help that evil, evil man destroy it. You heard him, he actually wants tigers to become extinct because it'll make him richer!" Polecat shook his head at the insanity of it. Surely everyone felt the same stirring in their guts when they saw a tiger? How could you not respect such a powerful, majestic beast? How could someone even think of hurting one?

"Polecat, we just have another day or so, then we'll be out of here, back to the forest. Fresh fruit, sleeping under the stars in our old hammocks. Fossa and Mako and Bear will all be there, we'll make fires, have our lessons, take it out on the aspirants. We'll be home."

Polecat rolled onto his back and looked at the ceiling. He so wanted to be home. Waking to the fluted tunes of the dawn chorus and the chattering of the squirrels, searching for fresh duck eggs at the start of spring and baking them in their shells. But how could it ever be the same again? Now that he knew all that horsing around was actually training to do such awful things? How could he take pride in treating a yew branch to make a bow, when he knew that same bow might loose an arrow on one of his fellow creatures?

"Close your eyes, Polecat, it will all make sense in the morning," Wolf said, and turned away. But Polecat knew sleep would not come so easily. In a way, Wolf would turn out to be right, but not in the way he imagined.

Just before first light, the two were shaken awake by Zhijan, the stately looking warrior who had greeted them on their arrival. He was clad in red martial arts robes with black trim and belt, and was carrying two sets of identical uniforms, one for each of them.

"I have been informed that you are both young masters in the fighting arts," he told them, "and that you would probably wish to study our methods. Here we train in the style of the Shaolin monks. Dawn training is about to begin."

The boys shook themselves awake, and splashed freezing water from the bedside basin into their faces to rouse themselves, then donned the uniforms and followed the warrior downstairs and into the courtyard. There they found about forty guards, all wearing identical uniforms, and with closely cropped haircuts. As the distant sun began to turn the tops of the highest summits around the valley pink and orange, the combatants lined up in a square, and took up the basic wide stance of the Shaolin. There was no instruction, no sensei or teacher taking charge. The soldiers had been practicing the same forms their whole lives. They ran through the movements with a dazzling synchronicity that Polecat and Wolf struggled to mirror. At essential points in the training, when the fighters needed to centre themselves and then punch or kick with all their force, they would shout in unison, channelling their ki, or life force, creating power in their strikes beyond that of a normal human. The shout was so guttural it seemed to come from the mountains itself, and sent a chill up the spines of the two Clan members.

Wolf was elated to be shaking the cobwebs from his under-exercised bones; this was the longest that he'd gone without physical training, and he was starting to feel sluggish and low. Polecat likewise forgot the concerns of the night and lost himself in his heartbeat and breathing, feeling the fluidity of the kung fu seethe through him as if he was nothing more than a conduit for the energy. As the training intensified, they moved into the five animal forms. First the monkey, movements becoming relaxed, almost playful, deceptive and unpredictable. Then the staccato robotic movements of the mantis, perfectly reflecting the striking style of that most accurate of insect assassins. As the morning light began to creep over the courtyard, throwing the shadows of the protagonists in stark relief across the ground, they took on the leaping, bounding grace of the crane, then the sinuous style of the snake, poised ready for a single, unbeatable strike. So much of the five styles spoke to Polecat of the very ethos of the Clan, the studied mirroring of animal abilities, learning from nature's deadly weapons, adapted to perfection not just over a thousand years of Shaolin years, but over millions of years of animal evolution. Polecat felt the grace of the crane sear through his veins, and the accuracy of the mantis become real in his clawed fists. But then, as the session reached its zenith, as they described the climax of animal perfection through their movements, the students curved their fingertips into claws, lips drew back into a snarl, and they seemed to grow in stature and power in the flicker of the dawn shadows. They had become the tiger. The style reflected that, for the Chinese, the tiger was king of beasts and the mountains. War tiger kung fu has no defensive moves, for the tiger fears nothing, and needs only attack. It is direct, simple, decisive and ferocious. The tiger claw techniques were swift and rounded, with an unearthly power like a big cat swiping. The nature of a tiger is never to retreat or surrender: a Chinese proverb says, "*When two tigers fight, one will die and the other will be severely wounded.*" So war tiger kung fu is indescribably brave and bold, lashing out with blows that must end your opponent's days before they end yours.

As Polecat's body swirled and lunged with the movements of the kung fu, his mind became free from thought. All he could feel was the power of the tiger coursing through him, commanding him like a puppet master. This martial art form was the fruition of a thousand years of respect, of study, of admiration for this majestic feline, and though it was designed to use the tiger's techniques to human advantage, actually it was the ultimate tribute, the ultimate sign of respect. When the class finished, the rest of the students relaxed, took time to stretch or chat with their fellows, perhaps to spar a little, but Polecat's mind was elsewhere. He walked up to the ramparts and looked over the valley, by now starting to boil with heat haze as the early morning sun scorched away the dew. He looked to the Himalayas for strength, and knew with absolute certainty that there was no way those tigers would be consigned to a fate with such loss of dignity. Not while he had breath in his body.

The sun too was burning away the icy fingers of the night from the world of Sinter and Saker. They had abandoned the Royal Enfield under the cover of some branches by the roadside, and hiked a small trail up a gorge between two summits towards a narrow col, which should lead over into the valley that housed Lang Chu. No human footprints had forged the way, just the cloven hooves of deer, taking the path of least resistance between feeding grounds. As so often, the deer had taken the easiest route while creating little real damage, allowing the pair to stay quite hidden among the intact undergrowth as they progressed. Each had to stop every few minutes to breathe as deeply as if they'd been running uphill rather than walking, the altitude burning away at their lungs. Within a few days they would have adjusted and created extra red blood cells to carry the sparse oxygen around their bodies. Until this acclimatisation process was in full swing, they would have to proceed with care or risk altitude sickness, which could be fatal.

They were pressing through unimaginably serene swaying bamboo groves. The bristling walls of the stems formed a cavern around them, slats of sun cutting down to them like divine light. The branches and leaves high above absorbed the sounds like heavy curtains, so that down on the dry forest floor it was eerily quiet. The stems of this mighty grass were in places as thick as a man's thigh – bamboo is one of the fastest growing plants on earth, growing as much as a metre in a day. But Saker was searching for a rather smaller stem. Eventually, he found one in diameter about equal to his own wrist, and using his knife, he chopped a piece of bamboo perhaps two metres long. Wedging the knife in the end cross-section of the bamboo, he carefully tapped the blade with a rock, and split the stem down its length. The inside was mainly hollow, apart from the nodes that split up the segments of the bamboo, which Saker cut out. He then used some rough sandpaper to make the groove down the centre of the bamboo smooth. Replacing the two halves of the bamboo together, he sealed them with some heated resin gathered from a nearby tree, and some twists of electrical tape. Next he took some thin slivers of bamboo and carved them into straight darts with pointed ends. Using twists of cotton wool at the end of each dart, he placed them on a line on the brown paper-like bamboo leaves that made a soft carpet beneath them.

"The perfect silent weapon," he told Sinter, as he filled an empty bag with water and hung it from a tree. He then paced out thirty steps, and placed one of the darts inside the bamboo tube. Putting his mouth to one end of the blowpipe, and pointing the other at the bag, he puffed out his cheeks and blew. Instantaneously the bag exploded with a pop, water burst in a flash of glittering sunlight, and dropped to the ground with a splash.

Sinter was delighted. "I want a go!"

Lunch done, they battled their way ever upwards, till they reached the col. Abruptly, the land fell away below them to the valley and the river, and perched exactly level with them across the river was the citadel of Lang Chu, squatting improbably on the mountainside like a crouching goblin. Sinter and Saker sat with a pair of binoculars, examining the citadel for most of the rest of the day. The road they had been driving on continued on the other side of the mountains, then cut through a narrow break in the peaks, passed over the river on a crumbly-looking concrete bridge, then wound its way right up to the city walls. The river itself was charged with glacial meltwater, and was a milky green colour, thundering down with extraordinary ferocity. It would be as cold as death, and was certainly not navigable. The only way across the river was the bridge, but there was a manned guard post at the end. And even if they'd been able to get past the guards, then how on earth did they get into the citadel? They could hardly just walk up to the gates and knock.

"I do have an idea," Saker said finally. "But it's very risky. And you're going to need a real head for heights."

Sinter didn't like the sound of that at all.

18

Sinter and Saker waited until night had spread its cloak over the valley, then dressed themselves in their old clothes, kindly altered by the Tibetan washerwoman. She had soaked them in black dye, so that now the two were clad like ninjas, dark scarves wound round their faces to cover their light skin as much as possible. Sinter took the rucksack. Saker wore the rope wound round him like a bandolier. In place of the boots they had brought for walking in the mountains, they wore simple plimsolls, as light as slippers so they could feel every pebble beneath their feet, allowing them to creep along as quietly as if they had been barefoot. They didn't tiptoe, though – tiptoeing places undue weight on the toes, creating more force to loudly crack twigs beneath them. Instead they placed the full foot down carefully, spreading their weight over as broad an area as possible; the same technique an elephant uses to allow its vast bulk to move in near silence.

Their eyes were soon used to the dark, and they made their way to the riverside, then crept along until they reached the struts of the bridge. Saker went up first, using the iron rivets poking from the concrete as if they were holds at a climbing wall, moving as easily and confidently as a gibbon. Sinter started up with similar ease, but as soon as she was more than head height from the ground, she looked down and was almost paralysed with fear. Suddenly she felt her heart race, and she gripped each bolt as if her life depended on it. Almost immediately she could feel her breathing start to quicken, her legs started to shudder and her forearms were pulsing with the effort. She fought not to scream in terror, she was running out of energy, she was going to fall! But then suddenly, Saker was beside her.

"Relax, Sinter," he told her quietly, in a soothing, easy voice. "The harder you hold, the more energy you will use, and the faster you will tire. I know it's hard, but take a deep breath, and take your time. If these rivets were just off the ground you could hang off them all day long, they are no smaller here . . . your brain is the only thing fighting you."

He was going to add, "Just let go!" but stopped himself in time.

Sinter closed her eyes, breathed in deeply, and allowed her muscles to go limp. "Concentrate, concentrate," she told herself.

Then ever so slowly and carefully, she started upwards,

Saker alongside her, coaching her every move.

"Watch where you're putting your toes," he told her. "Accuracy is everything. Focus on the hold you're going for, and don't stop looking at it until your foot is set there . . . yes! That's it!"

His easy confidence encouraged the same in her, and before she knew it, they were sitting on the horizontal iron beam of the bridge, high above the water, legs hanging over the rushing tumult. Now they had to cross the beams underneath the whole length of the bridge, their heads just metres below the road. Saker made it look so easy, almost dancing around the upright struts, hanging over the water with a single hand holding onto the ironwork. Sinter on the other hand hugged her way around every obstacle. Again, it would have been easy at ground level, but up here any slip would mean a lethal drop to the icy carnage below. She mustn't think of that, she just mustn't!

About halfway along the bridge, Sinter was finally beginning to find her nerve. She had crossed probably the width of a playing field, and was starting to think she might actually reach the other side. Saker waited for her to catch up over a short section, then turned to push on, and pulled a chunk of rust right off the top of one of the struts, losing his handhold, and swinging right out over the river. Sinter yelled, and grabbed his shirt, pulling him back in, swinging them both further under the bridge, where they crashed their heads into a tangle of twigs hanging there. Instantly, with a panicked cacophony of "sree sree" cries, a phalanx of swallows thundered from their nests and took wing, their feathers skimming Sinter's face and hair. Saker thrashed out with his free hand in panic as the flood of birds swirled into the air. Finally all the birds had flown, their calls still audible as they circled over the water in confusion. The kerfuffle had attracted the attention of the guards above, and as Sinter and Saker crouched in total silence, too terrified to move, they could hear frantic footfalls above them, as the soldiers converged on the source of the mayhem. The guards turned on a high-powered torch, and leaned over the balustrade of the bridge, turning its beam on the source of the commotion. The yellow light searched along the beam that Sinter and Saker had been walking, casting eerie shadows down its length, playing around the plimsolls of the hiding pair. They held their breath, fingers crossed, wishing the beams to pass them by and the soldiers to move on. They could hear the soldiers arguing, and for a second the beam seemed to alight on one of Saker's shoes. They could hear muffled conversation, the guards making up their minds. Were they going to come down and investigate? But then the light was flicked off, and they heard the shuffling of feet as the guards walked away. Someone had decided they had got excited over nothing, and they were heading back to the nice warm guard house and the bottle of hot rice wine they were sharing inside. Saker and Sinter breathed out.

"You just saved my life," Saker seriously told Sinter. "I owe you one now."

"Get me to the other side of this bridge," said Sinter, "and we'll call it evens."

Descending, with the ground getting ever closer, was somehow easier than going up, and within minutes they were on solid ground, breathing hard, but knowing they had barely begun. Now, instead of heading towards the gates of the citadel, they made their way to the cliff-face that led almost vertically to the ramparts, high, high above. This was the risky bit that Saker had been talking about. He took the rope from his shoulders, and tied one end round his waist in a simple belt. The other end of the rope he formed into several twists, creating leg loops and a waistband to make a harness for Sinter.

"There's a small ledge about twenty metres up," he said, "I'll get to there then bring you up. And remember, don't look down!"

He slung the rucksack and bamboo over his shoulder, wiped the undersoles of his plimsolls, making sure there was no grit or dirt to foil the friction and ruin his grip. Then he wiped his forehead on his sleeve, and his hands on his trousers. He took a sharp breath, shook his head to focus, and took hold of the rock face.

The rock was ancient limestone, and held his fingertips well, but it was terrifyingly steep. There was a reason this side of the citadel was not watched; what fool would try and climb here? And at night time?

"I must be off my head," Saker hissed to himself through gritted teeth.

There was just enough pale moonlight for them to make out the small imperfections in the rock that would make hand- and foot-holds, but it would take enormous concentration. Saker adored climbing, and had the perfect build and temperament for it, yet even he found this hard going. He quickly began to regret having even thought of bringing Sinter up here. Surely she wouldn't be able to manage something so challenging on her first proper climb? As this thought zipped into his head, a chunk of loose limestone popped off under his foot, sending his body swinging out over the void. Luckily his handholds were solid, and he swung back into the rock face, breathing heavily, as Sinter dodged the falling chunk of rock below and it burst into a thousand pieces. When his feet touched the cliff again, he puffed and panted with fright and exertion, but focused on his breathing, forcing it to slow and relax. Ever so gently he continued, now checking every foot- and hand-hold with a little tug before he'd commit his weight to it. At the ledge, he sat down, bracing one foot sideways against a rock. He took in the free rope, and passed the spare rope around his waist and over the shoulder, in an old-fashioned Alpine brace. As Sinter climbed, he would take in the slack; if she slipped, he might be able to restrain her. If however she took a big fall, her weight would pull both of them to their deaths.

From the ground, Sinter repeated Saker's mantra before

setting off. She had to wipe her hands four times before she felt she'd got them free of sweat. She couldn't put this off forever, and took a hold of the rock, breathing out hard.

"Come on," she told herself, "get your head together!"

No sooner had she started, though, than Sinter found her rhythm. She was considerably lighter than Saker, and now that she was relatively relaxed, she progressed with much more ease. Saker looked down, and noted with relief that Sinter was taking the weight on the larger stronger muscles of her legs and feet, and preserving her weaker hands and forearms.

He remembered that when Clan members first learned to climb they'd been told that inexperienced men have a tendency to try and macho chin-up their way up climbs and thus burn out in seconds. Girls on the other hand are much more subtle, and instinctively take their weight on their legs and feet, and therefore tend to pick up climbing more quickly than boys. Sinter was proving this to be true, and was without doubt a natural. Before Saker knew it, she was alongside him on the ledge, breathing hard, but with a smile on her face born of exhilaration.

"That was incredible, you flew up that!" he told her. "But this next bit is hardest, make sure you let that rope pay out freely or it'll snag and I'll be in big trouble." And then he thought hard, paused and addressed her seriously. "Actually, I think you should take the harness off until I'm safe."

Sinter looked at him aghast. "What? Why? Isn't the rope keeping us safe?"

"Well, it's pretty good when I'm bringing you up and reeling you in from above. But I weigh much more than you. If I fall off you won't be able to catch me. I'll simply pull you off too, and then . . ."

He left his sentence hanging. He didn't need to finish it. Sinter looked over the edge to the rocks way below, then at the knots around her waist. She took the knot in her hand as if to undo it, but then tied an extra double knot in it.

"No way," she said with finality. "We're in this together. You risk your life for me, I risk mine for you. That's the deal when you're a team." And then she added, "Just don't fall."

Saker again went through his routine, rubbing grit off the bottom of his plimsolls, wiping his hands, breathing out to centre himself. Then ran his hands over the rock, looking for a hand-hold. He could feel himself shivering with the effort, his heart beating so hard it seemed to thump in his ears. He had to talk to himself, repeating all the advice he'd just given Sinter: "lightness of touch, come on, don't grip it like grim death". He was increasingly aware that he'd been on the ledge, looking for the move that would take him away from safety for too long. He was putting it off, his present position was becoming too comfortable. If he stayed much longer he would never go. Soon he'd start freaking Sinter out, and it would become even harder for him to make the move away from the security he currently felt. He closed his eyes, gently butted his head on the rock, gritted his teeth and started up. The climb felt as if it was more than vertical, and he could feel the lactic acid building in his forearms, deadening his sensation, setting his muscles quivering with effort. For the first time in his life, Saker could not look down, the dizzying distance below him sent his stomach whirling, and made him want to whimper with terror. Perhaps ten minutes after stepping away from Sinter, he was still well below the ramparts, and there was little or nothing left in his fingers. Sweat poured from his face as his leg started to wobble vigorously . . . he was going to fall! With his whole body quivering he thrashed around, frantically seeking a hold he knew he would not find. But then his fingers found an empty space. A hole! In fact a big gaping gap big enough for him to push his whole arm into up to the elbow. He gripped the inside of it, and shook his other hand, allowing the blood to rush back to it, and the lactic acid to subside. As strength returned to it, he swapped arms and repeated the procedure. He could feel his power afresh, enough to get him to the underside of the ramparts. When he finally took a grip of the stonework, the relief was so intense that he could have cried. Instead he just breathed out the fear and stress, and eased himself up fractionally so he could look over the edge.

Beyond the battlement was a courtyard, illuminated

only by flickering flaming torches. At first glance he thought it was empty, but then he stiffened. At the back of the courtyard was a building with wooden doors, and shuttered windows leaking a little light. As Saker's eyes got used to the gleam, he saw an armoured soldier slouching against the wall, arms crossed, a long pike in the crook of his elbow. He was so motionless; perhaps he was asleep? After a minute's watching, Saker saw him scratch his nose. Infinitesimally slowly, Saker reached over his shoulder and slid the bamboo pole from where it was tied to his rucksack. With one hand still holding the rampart, and his toes teetering on the tiniest of ledges, he forced himself not to think of the vast gulf beneath him, or the fact that he was still tied to Sinter. He steadied his hand, raised the pole to his lips, took aim, and blew. Instantly, the guard's hand flew up to his neck. A direct hit! The soldier clearly thought he had been stung by some biting insect, and scratched at his neck. If he'd thought more carefully he'd have realised that very few insects manage to stay active at this height and in temperatures this cold. However, this clearly didn't enter his mind, and as the bamboo dart had not stayed in his neck, but merely nicked him then fallen to the floor, he soon lost interest and slumped back against the wall. Now Saker knew it was only a matter of time.

After five minutes, it seemed Saker's toes were being stabbed with ice picks, his calf muscles were wobbling incessantly, and his fingers trembled not just with cold but with near total exhaustion. Just when it seemed he could hold on no longer, and he would have to clamber over and give himself up, the guard started to sway. He bent at the waist as if cramped, wiped foaming white spit from his mouth, then fell to his knees and plopped face-first on to the flagstones.

Saker crawled over the ramparts, and finally stood on solid ground. He waited just long enough to get his breath back, then pulled in the slack rope, took the strain round his waist, and gave two tugs to signal to Sinter that she should start to climb. These were nervous moments, standing out in the open hauling in the rope, praying that nobody came into the courtyard. Sinter, though, was by now warming to her task, and practically skipped up the remaining metres of rock. The sound of her efforts scrabbling below drifted up to Saker on the still night air, and he silently willed her to climb a little more quietly, expecting any second to have a burly hand slap down on his shoulder. Finally she fell over the edge, and gave Saker a huge hug of relief.

"We made it, I can't believe we made it!" Looking over his shoulder, she saw the soldier crumpled on the ground, and managed to muffle a shriek of horror. "What did you do? What did you do?" She ran softly across to the man, discarding the rope as she went.

"How could you do this? I thought you were going to change!"

"It's OK, Sinter," Saker pleaded, "He's not dead, he's

out cold. I used crushed laburnum petals on the darts. Too much and it can be fatal, but just enough and it results in unconsciousness, it's temporary, and he'll come around no worse for wear. Well, he'll feel rotten but he'll be fine."

As quietly as they could, they dragged the soldier behind a giant vase and propped him in the shadows where he wouldn't be spotted, then gently pushed open the door and stepped inside.

The corridor was illuminated by burning torches, dancing yellow sprites over ancient paintings of serpentine dragons in faded oranges and greens. Long yellowing scrolls of bamboo canvas hung to the ground, emblazoned with beautifully painted Chinese characters, and images of waterfalls, forests and mighty beasts. Wooden doors every few metres led into endless rooms. There were no windows, and no other means of looking inside. As they progressed, Sinter's courage faltered. They could never investigate the rooms behind every one of these doors. The citadel was vast, how on earth would they ever find the tigers?

At the end of the corridor they took a staircase that led down, the walls now carved from the rock of the mountain itself. At the bottom of the staircase they found a most incongruous sight, a shiny metal door, with metal rivets running around the edge. Saker pulled Sinter back as she stepped towards it, and pointed to a closed circuit camera that was aimed at the space in front of the door.

"What on earth are we going to do now?" she hissed at him.

Suddenly they heard the sound of footfalls behind them.

There was nowhere for them to go, they were trapped.

19

"**W**ouldn't you know it," a voice said from the shadows behind them. "You travel half the continent, get to within metres, and then hit a dead end. What are the chances?"

Saker stepped in front of Sinter as it to protect her, but she stepped to his side in a futile gesture of solidarity. Whatever they were facing now they would face together.

"Who says it's a dead end," said Saker, "I hope for your sake there's more than just the one of you – we're not done yet!"

"I don't doubt it," said the dark shape as he stepped out into the light.

"You!" Sinter hissed.

"Yes, me," said Polecat, running his hand over his stubbly head and turning to Saker. "I can't believe you managed to find us here, that's . . . pretty impressive."

"The Prophet named me because I don't give up easily,"

Saker whispered, the threat audible in his tone.

"It was the same for me, Saker." Polecat stood to face his opponent head on, shoulders squared, ready to defend against any attack.

"Really? So what the hell have we been doing with our lives? Do you remember following animals for days on end, learning about how they work? When did that all become about hurting animals for money? What happened to the respect? What the hell do you think we're doing here, Polecat?"

"The Clan is supposed to be all about the wild world," Sinter interjected. "You've totally sold out everything you're supposed to believe in!"

"You don't know anything about what I believe in," Polecat retorted, "and as far as hurting animals for money . . . you have no idea." Something about his tone made the pair stop short.

"This place is evil," said Polecat. "I want no part of what goes on here." There was an air of both sadness and fortitude in his voice now. Saker's fists were clenched tight, but began to ease.

"Lang Chu is in the command of a warlord called the Gong," Polecat continued. "He makes millions in the illegal animal trade – tigers are just the tip of the iceberg. And the cubs? They're going to be farmed for their body parts. The whole thing is just sick."

Sinter stepped forward, reaching out to him. "Polecat, you know this is wrong. We've given everything to get here and do something about this, you *have* to help us."

Polecat stepped back, unsure. "If I help you," he began, "I'll be an outcast; like you." He nodded at Saker. "I'll never be able to go back to the forest, I'll be on the run. A nothing. All I want is for it all to be over, and for things to go back to how they used to be."

"That can never happen now," Sinter said. "Everything is different now. How could you go back and play at being Clan, when you know what's behind that door?"

"And what else am I supposed to do?" he spat at her. "The Clan is all I know, I'm happy there. I just want it all to be over," he repeated.

The tension was fearsome. At any second Polecat could have shouted out, and it would have all been over.

"Look, perhaps there is a way," Sinter faltered. "Get us through that door, help us to find the tigers and get them out of there, then just run, head back to your bed, pretend you never saw us. They'd take you back then, wouldn't they? You'd have helped us, the tigers would be free, and you'd be back in the forest in a matter of days."

Polecat cocked his head at her, working things out. "You wouldn't tell anyone? If you get caught, you won't tell them I helped you?"

"You have my word," said Sinter.

"Mine too," added Saker, holding his hand out to his Clan brother. Polecat looked at it with distrust, but then held out his own hand and shook.

The three crouched in the shadows and hatched their plan. Polecat talked them through the layout of the citadel and the tunnels ahead, and told them how the doors could be opened.

"Where are the guards monitoring these cameras?" Saker asked.

"Just beyond this door, there'll probably only be one at this time of night," came the answer.

Saker nibbled his upper lip. "Do you think they'd let you through?"

Polecat nodded.

Saker took the blowpipe darts from round his waist and gave one to his Clan brother. The rest he took himself.

"If you can take the guard out with this, then open every door between the tigers and the outside, your job is done," he told him. And then, before they set their plan in action, Saker asked for one more piece of information. "There's one more location I need."

He turned to Sinter. "I will meet you in the storeroom in ten minutes. If I'm not there by then, release the tigers and run, never look back, don't ever think of me again."

This time Sinter didn't argue. She nodded. There was more at stake now than either of them as individuals. Before he ran off, Saker turned to Polecat and clasped him in a firm hug. They didn't say anything. They didn't need to.

Saker trotted back down the corridor, his feet padding gently on the wooden floorboards. He ducked behind a column as two soldiers emerged from one of the doors, chatting. He stood impossibly still as they walked past him and in through another door, then after a few seconds he ran softly out to the courtyard. Polecat's directions had pointed him to a room on the second storey, so he sprang lightly onto a windowsill, swung from a beam above him, and danced up the side of the building till he could lever himself on to a window ledge. Man-made buildings are, he thought, often so much easier to climb than rock faces! He dropped in to a corridor that was the mirror image of the one below, lined with closed wooden doors and elaborate paintings. This time, though, he knew exactly which door he was looking for. Quietly he bounded down the hallway, counting the doors as he went. As he rounded a corner expecting to find the entrance he needed, he saw a guard was standing outside it. This soldier was alert, staring straight ahead with a concentration that spoke of great discipline. Hidden by the corner, Saker crouched, took his blowpipe in his hand and loaded a dart. Painstakingly slowly, he lifted the pipe to his lips, leant around the corner, and blew.

There was a "ping" as the dart hit the guard's helmet and bounced off. Saker ducked back, holding his breath, pressing back against the wall and willing himself to become invisible.

"Step out of the shadows, boy." A voice summoned him, "It's time."

Saker sighed, placed his blowpipe on the ground, and prepared to face his foe.

Polecat nodded to Sinter, and she shrank into the darkness. He swelled his chest, threw back his head to show the utmost confidence, and sauntered right round to the door. The security camera swung to look at him, like the eyes of an attentive robot. He looked up at the camera, and raised a hand in greeting to the invisible watchers beyond. A tense second followed, then the door slid open. It took a few seconds for his eyes to adjust to the unnatural light in the tunnel beyond. The electric lights cast no shadows for the boy to hide in, from here on in it all had to be overt, handled with confidence and bluster. He walked to the guard post. As he'd predicted, only one man was at the deck of monitors keeping an eye on comings and goings throughout the depths of the citadel. He stood as Polecat approached. "What are you doing down here this time of night? No one told me anything about this!"

"Oh, really?" said Polecat nonchalantly, "The Gong told me I could come down any time. I couldn't sleep, so I thought I'd come have a look at the animals."

"Don't give me that!" the guard responded, "I'm going to have to call someone down here to deal with this." Polecat nodded, and motioned to the telephone on the guard's desk, indicating that he should feel free to do as he wished. As soon as the guard had turned his back, Polecat leapt forward, jabbing him in the neck with the blowpipe dart.

"Hey!" called out the guard in surprise, grabbing at his

neck. Polecat clasped his hand over the guard's mouth as he fought to shout, and wrapped himself around the bigger man like his weasely namesake, clasping his body with tireless clawing hands. The guard flailed, but Polecat was always just out of reach, climbing all over him like a stoat taking on a rabbit many times its size. Finally the man stumbled over his own feet and tripped. Polecat clambered onto his back, his hand still clamped over the man's mouth. The more the man struggled, the more his heart raced, carrying the poison around his bloodstream. Within minutes, he started to tire, foam began to dribble from his mouth, and his blows became less and less potent. Polecat hung on, as if trying to squeeze him into submission. Eventually the toxin took full effect, and the guard fell unconscious. Polecat hung on for another minute just to be safe, then rolled away exhausted. He lay on his back gasping, then whistled to Sinter, who came rushing in.

"Are you all right?" she asked him, surveying the scene.

"I'll be a damn sight better when I'm away from you two. Come on, follow me."

He vanished down the rocky passageway, ignoring all the side entrances that led off into other parts of the complex. Sinter shuddered to think what horrors lurked there in the guts of the mountain, but she had come here to save the cubs. The Gong's other activities could not distract her from that. Finally they reached the holding cave. Sinter cried out with instant heartbreak. She made as if to go up to the bars, but Polecat grabbed her arm and held her back.

"These aren't pussycats, Sinter, don't think that just because they're caged they're helpless."

Sinter stepped back, taking his advice, but then spied a familiar box. Her next shriek was with glee – the cubs! She ran over to the box, and opened the lid. Two familiar sleepy forms mewed up at her, recoiling slightly from the harsh light after the darkness of their prison. Sinter was filled with delight.

"It's all right, little ones, we're going to get you out of here," she told them earnestly. "Nobody's going to hurt you again."

"What are you going to do with them?" Polecat asked. "It's a full-time job bringing up a pair of tiger cubs, you know."

"I have no idea," Sinter replied. "First we get them out of this awful place, then we can start thinking about the future."

"Yeah, I was kind of noticing you don't think much beyond the next day, do you?" he replied with an air of both reproach and respect.

"If you stopped to consider the outcome of everything you did, you'd never do anything."

Then she quoted a famous Buddhist saying, known to pretty much any school kid on the subcontinent: "Do not pursue the past. Do not lose yourself in the future. The past no longer is. The future has not yet come."

He nodded his understanding and indicated a metal lever on the wall.

"That lever there will lift all the doors to the tigers' cages. When the time comes, pull it, and then make sure you're well behind the cages. With any luck they'll bolt for the exit. I'll make sure their way out is open . . . I can't wait to see how the citadel will cope with having six angry tigers on the loose! How you get out after that . . . well, that's your business. I hope I can trust you to keep your side of the bargain."

As he turned to go, Sinter called out to him. "Polecat. You've done the right thing here tonight. Thank you." He half snorted a reply to her, and then was gone.

20

Saker's adversary removed his helmet, revealing striking features. He stood a hand span taller than the boy. Saker knew from his lightness of step and the sway of his shoulders that he was a man used to combat, a warrior. He was not to know it was Zhijan, the same guard who had guided Polecat and Wolf around the citadel. Zhijan unbuckled the crossed swords from his back and propped them against the wall, drew back his sleeves in a classic martial arts posture. Saker paced out to face him, then stepped back with his right foot, taking up a defensive posture, offering the smallest possible target to his opponent. "Aren't you going to shout for your boss? Why not call the tiger killer out here to face me himself?"

"You are the boy Saker." It was not a question, but a matter-of-fact statement. It was as if Zhijan knew everything! "You travelled far to come here, young man. You have proved yourself worthy of my respect. There is no need to involve anyone else in this."

Saker hitched up his trousers to allow room and comfort to kick, and centred himself, preparing for the onslaught.

"How can you take the tiger stance, when your life is all about killing tigers? Where is your respect?"

"This is the way of nature," replied his opponent. "Tigers were the ultimate predator. Now the ultimate predator is man. We learned from the animals, and now we rule over them. If they die out, it is evolution, that is the natural way."

With that, he took on the clawed hands of the warrior tiger techniques, and struck at his young opponent.

Saker ducked and weaved away, gasping at the unerring ferocity of the attack. He was forced backwards, parrying blows one by one, almost battered into submission at the very first attack. It was pointless taking on the warrior on his terms. Instead, Saker reacted with an instinctive move from aikido, or the way of harmonious spirit, redirecting his opponent's energy and using it against them. Aikido is particularly effective when the attacker is bigger, stronger and charging head on in unfettered aggression.

As Zhijan struck, Saker palmed his blow away and kept on moving, describing a big circle, slipping his hips under the bodyweight of the bigger man, throwing him off balance and sending him sprawling to the floor.

Zhijan instantly rolled back to his feet and nodded with appreciation, but just as instantly was back on the attack. There was no time for Saker to formulate a strategy, but he instinctively knew that if the tiger has one weakness, it is that its method of attacking through all-out explosive brutality, combined with its size and weight, means that it uses all its energy rapidly, then fatigues. If its attack did not bear fruit within seconds, the animal would tire, and become vulnerable. It was the same with tiger kung fu. Saker just kept side-stepping and parrying the ceaseless blows, saving what remained of his energy for when Zhijan showed a weakness.

Finally, the guard overextended himself in a strike and put himself very slightly off balance.

Saker saw his opportunity. Blocking the fist, he swivelled and struck at Zhijan's elbow, pressing it in a direction elbows just don't like to go. He used his entire body weight to press against this pressure point, and spun around Zhijan, drawing him in a big circle, finally taking his feet from under him, forcing him face-first to the ground, with his arm twisted uncomfortably in an armlock.

"Well done, boy, your teacher must be very proud of your abilities."

"I don't think he would be, if he knew what I was about to do," Saker puffed through his hectic breathing. "Now, there's something you can do to help me."

The Gong woke up to the door of his room being thrown open, and Zhijan walking stiffly inside.

"What is the meaning of this, Zhijan?" he demanded.

But instead of responding, Zhijan stared vacantly ahead, foam bubbling from his lips. Then he fell to the ground, incapacitated by some powerful toxin. Behind him a lithe young man stepped forward.

"Wolf?" the Gong, only half-awake, asked. "What are you doing?"

"I'm not Wolf," said the boy, "I'm a far more lethal beast. My name is Saker, and I'm here to talk to you about your business."

The Gong sat up in his bed, feeling vulnerable in his nightshirt, blinking away sleep with the new light. "You're the boy that went rogue. The Clan boy! How did you find your way here?"

"That is not your concern. I have come for the tigers. And I'm here to tell you that your trade in tigers has to end. Now."

"What exactly is it you think you can threaten me with, boy? You will never escape from here alive."

"That may be so, but I have already called the authorities in Beijing. They are probably on their way even now, and when they find what you've been up to here, you will go to prison for a thousand lifetimes."

The Gong actually laughed aloud. "What, do you think for a second the party leaders don't know what goes on here? Who do you think drinks the majority of my tiger wine? Nice bluff, boy, but I have protection you could never dream of. You think you frighten me because you can find your way into my castle? You are nothing, a hiccup at best."

"I broke in once, I can do it again," Saker responded with quiet confidence, "and you will always be watching your back, always. I will be listening, and if I hear you have so much as traded in a single tiger skin, I will be back here to find you, and next time the poison I bring will be one you won't wake up from."

With that, he jabbed the Gong in the neck with his last remaining dart, then leapt onto his chest, and clapped his hand over his mouth until he succumbed to the toxin.

It was with total relief that Sinter finally heard footsteps coming down the passageway towards her. It had to be Saker at last; they could finish their task and finally set the tigers free. She walked over to the lever that released the cages, and took it in her hand. "What kept you?" she called out sarcastically as he padded into the room.

"Sinter?" an astounded voice responded.

She glanced round in disbelief. At the entrance to the storeroom stood not Saker, but a man in a white suit she instantly recognised.

"Doctor Arjun! What are you doing here?" she almost screamed.

Had her father sent him to rescue her? Had he come here on some misguided attempt to save his betrothed? But that didn't make any sense, how could he have followed her?

"I might well ask you the same thing," he replied, and then said with a loud sigh, "my dear, you have certainly shown more spirit than I could possibly have imagined."

"If you're here to rescue me, you can forget it, I don't need rescuing, I'm here to release the tigers."

"I'm afraid I can't let you do that, Sinter," he replied. "My business with the Gong is much too precious for that. Those cages hold several million dollars worth of investment."

As he spoke, another figure entered the room. For a second Sinter saw the stubbly hair and build, but it wasn't Saker, it was Wolf.

"There is just no way . . ." Wolf began as he saw Sinter.

He made to leap forward towards her, but Sinter motioned to pull the lever, and Wolf suddenly saw the awful potential of what would happen should she release the tigers.

"No! You stay right where you are," Sinter said. "Either you tell me what's going on, or I'll pull this lever, and the two of you are going to be tiger food. I should do it anyway!"

Wolf and Doctor Arjun looked at each other, as if making up their minds what to do and say. Eventually the white-suited man shrugged, and began his story. "It is true that I am a doctor, but I have not run a surgery for a long time. I found out many years ago that there is a much more lucrative way to make a living. I provide the Gong with animals from the north of India, and he provides me with clients, and pays me handsomely."

"You?!" she demanded, horrified. "I always knew you were a horrible man, you just wait till Papaji finds out about this!"

Despite his predicament, Arjun could not contain a

slight guffaw at Sinter's outburst. "Sinter, how do you think your father manages to live so well on a tea estate? Tea is not the commodity it used to be! Your father and I have been business partners for years now. He gave you to me as a present for all the money I've brought him over the years . . . I'm sorry that you had to hear about it like this, but this is the real world. This is how it is. When you have grown up a bit, you will understand."

He made to move towards her, and instantly Sinter pulled down slightly on the lever, the cage doors creaked upwards, flecks of rust tumbled off the iron gates and the slumbering tigers leapt to their feet, snarling. Arjun stepped back, holding his hands up to placate her. It was Wolf who spoke.

"Sinter, think a second. If you pull that lever the tigers will be free for a few minutes, but they can't get out of the citadel. It would be too hard to catch them, so the guards will shoot them."

"We thought of that," Sinter responded, "all the doors to the outside world are open. The tigers may not all get away, but some will, and that's better than them ending up in a soup to line your filthy pockets."

"You're not going to pull that lever," Wolf said calmly, "because it's not like pulling the trigger of a gun. These are wild animals, let them free and you do not know what they will do. They might turn and take you, they might take your precious Saker. The second you pull the lever, you have no control. You're not going to pull it."

"Yes, she will," said another voice. Saker had made his way down from the Gong's room, and entered the room quietly. "Do it, Sinter, show them what we came here for."

She stared at him in terror. Now they were all standing in the firing line, and what Wolf had said was totally true. Though she wanted the tigers free and Arjun punished, the second she let them loose she lost control. She didn't really want to see anybody killed, and certainly not Saker. She couldn't do it. Defeated, her body slumped, and momentarily she slackened her grasp.

Wolf saw his chance and made to pounce, but instinctively Sinter pulled the lever. The gates sprang up, and the tigers leapt into action as if they'd been given an electric shock. Three surged down the corridor, one leapt straight at Wolf, who dropped to the ground and it pounced clear over his head. Another stopped dead as it found Doctor Arjun's bulk in its way. It snarled with an intensity which set the hairs up on the back of the neck, its ears flattened against its head as it swiped several times at the quaking Doctor, and bounded past him. Arjun fell to his knees with his hands clasped round his head, as if praying the whole nightmare would end.

Then there was an unnatural silence, apart from the distant sounds of echoing snarls, and human screams of shock and terror. Everyone looked around them, expecting to see shredded human remains . . . but there was nothing. Miraculously, everyone had escaped unharmed. Wolf raised himself to his full height, and turned to face Saker.

"Now is the reckoning, Saker. You have destroyed me in the eyes of the Prophet, you have wrecked my chances of leading the Clan, and I'm going to make you pay."

Saker took up his defensive stance, but he knew it was useless. Even when Saker was at his best, Wolf was stronger. But now? Now that he had just been through the hardest fight of his life, not to mention climbing the rock face and the previous three days of hardship and effort; Saker knew he had no chance. As the two boys faced off, he could see Wolf's confidence. He was fresh, he was prepared, and he was angry. He would be swift and merciless.

But then Sinter called out, "Saker! The basket!"

Saker followed the direction of her pointing finger to the bundles of contraband. There were several woven baskets that looked just like those snake charmers use all over India. Saker instantly understood what she was suggesting. He leapt towards them as Wolf lunged in for his first attack, Saker yanked a basket down onto the floor, where the lid rolled free, tipping the contents out. Instantly, the vast snake that had been interned within reared, standing a full metre off the ground in classic threat posture. It was a king cobra, the largest and longest venomous snake in the world, and as its vast bulk slithered from the basket, it became evident that it was near five metres in length, and as broad as a man's calf.

Snake charmers may play sounds through various flutes and other instruments when they "charm" cobras, but actually the snakes are not reacting to the sounds at all.

They have no external ear openings, and perceive sounds by lying their heads on the ground, and letting vibrations be transmitted to the jaw. In actual fact they are responding to the swaying motions of the snake charmer. Cobras are utterly dependent on vision, and will always turn their attention to movement. This is particularly evident when they are frightened, and are trying to intimidate someone they consider threatening. As Wolf lunged towards Saker, his movements meant he instantly became the primary focus for the giant snake, which swung round and struck out. Wolf just managed to dodge back in terror, the strike missing him by a matter of centimetres. Arjun and Sinter gasped with horror.

"King cobras don't like people," Saker finally spoke. "They live in deep forests miles away from us, and when they see us they either flee, or if they can't do that they'll stand their ground. This one has nowhere to go, it feels cornered, and if you move, it's going to bite you."

"Is it deadly?" stammered Arjun.

"Not usually to us," Wolf answered calmly, though the sweat was pouring down his forehead. "But it has one of the highest venom yields of all snakes."

"Bites have killed people in just over a minute," added Saker, as the snake again reared to its full height and lunged at Wolf, with a hiss that was so guttural, it almost sounded like a growl. Wolf and Saker had heard that sound before. King cobras have special membranes in the back of the throat that create this monstrous sound, designed for moments such as now when they need a potential enemy to know they are dangerous and best left alone. Even an elephant will flee the terrifying display of the king, and not surprisingly as theoretically the snake has enough venom to kill an elephant.

"Sinter," Saker addressed her as quietly as he could manage, "walk around behind the snake, as slowly and carefully as you can, head for the door."

As she started, Wolf made to move towards her, but his movement caught the majestic snake's attention, and it reared and struck. Dr Arjun again cringed backwards, covering his head with his hands. Saker and Sinter, now carrying the box with the cubs in it, edged their way towards the exit.

"Where do you think you're going to go, Saker?" Wolf called out evenly. "You are nothing without the Clan, you won't last a day in the outside world, you have no contacts, no friends, you'll be nothing."

"I've lasted this long," Saker retorted.

"And he has one friend," Sinter added.

Wolf snorted in derision. "You're both dreaming. You won't even make it out of the citadel. And if you do, there is nothing but the Himalayas. Where do you think you're going to hide? The Clan will find you within the week."

"Maybe so," Saker responded, "but I'll have done what you never could, Wolf. When you start thinking for yourself, and working out the horror you're mixed up in, come find us."

With that the pair turned, and sprinted down the passageway. They heard Wolf's final threat ringing in their ears: "Keep running, Saker, we're never going to let you rest. Never. You'll always be running!"

21

Saker and Sinter raced along the corridor, at any moment expecting to turn a corner and see a closed door, or armed soldiers blocking their way. However Polecat had been true to his word – every gateway was wide open. As for the guards, they had all fled in panic at the cavalcade of cats that had stampeded out in search of escape. There was no point in skulking in the shadows now. They emerged from the rocky passageway, ran across the courtyard and down into the temple. They lumbered under the weight of the cubs, following the distant sounds of carnage, across the main square, where the two helicopters stood eerily shining in the moonlight. As they ran past them, Saker stopped abruptly, then ran up and swung open the door of the first chopper. Unbelievably, the keys were in the ignition!

For one wonderful moment Sinter's heart leapt. "Don't tell me you know how to fly one of these?"

Saker looked at her with wry humour. "Er, no, can you?"

Her response was a look that could have stripped paint. Saker grinned, then pulled the keys out of the ignition, and with all his might threw them out over the balustrade.

"That's one chopper that won't be chasing us!"

He ran to the second helicopter. This time the keys were not so readily evident. He scrabbled around looking for a place the pilot might have thought to leave them,

"Come on, come on!" shouted Sinter with urgency, "they're going to be here any minute!" Abandoning the search, Saker merely reached down behind the console, and grabbed handfuls of wires, yanked with all his might, pulling them from their sockets, hoping to cause some kind of damage to the whirlybird.

"If in doubt, yank stuff out!" he quipped, as he pulled another fistful of wires.

They sped across the square and headed into the narrow streets of the village. People were running about everywhere shouting and screaming, and the place was in total chaos. Sinter grabbed Saker by the arm, just in time to stop him being broadsided by a tiger as it leapt out of the open door of one of the houses. Inside, a woman wailed in terror. They followed the tiger as it bounded down the cobbled street, joining a throng of people rushing confused in the half-light.

Now the shout went up from soldiers scattered by the feline furore, as they picked themselves up and realised the pair charging past them were not locals. One armoured man gripped his pike and took up position in the centre of the street, facing the pair in a seemingly impenetrable barrier.

Saker didn't pause for a second, but leapt sideways towards the walls lining the street, bounced off the wall at waist height, launching himself up over the pike blade, and above the head of the guard. As the guard cocked his head back, his helmet wedged on the back of his armour and he started to topple backwards. Saker caught his head, and then twisted in mid air, landing back to back with the guard. He continued twisting as he moved, throwing the guard elegantly over his shoulder and sending him crashing on the cobbles.

It seemed impossible that Polecat could have made it all the way down here and opened the main gateway to the walled city, but in actuality it hadn't been necessary. As soon as the tigers went on the rampage inside the walls, the locals had hammered on the gateway, demanding that the doors be thrown open, and the beasts released into the night. Having to react at the business end of the world's most fearsome set of canines, the guards had instantly thrown the doors open and allowed the cats to flee across the bridge, where they would doubtless scare the living daylights out of the guards enjoying their hot rice wine.

But what now? Wolf had been right, the tigers might well disappear in the bamboo forests of the surrounding hills, but Saker and Sinter would be tracked and caught.

How on earth could they make good their escape? Just then, Sinter saw several huge wheel-shaped straw bales propped against the walls of a house.

"Saker, here, help me," she called.

He had no idea what she was proposing, but had no plans himself, so ran to her aid.

Sinter placed the box with the cubs on the ground, and levered a wheel of straw off the wall. The second it was no longer wedged against the wall, the downhill gradient of the street started the wheel rolling. At first it was extremely slow, but soon it started to build momentum.

"Now run!" yelled Sinter, picking up the box, and starting after the trundling bale. Pushing it from behind, they managed to get it rolling at quite a pace, and soon it was plummeting towards the gateway. As it approached, the guards shouted for them to stop, and drew their pikes, but it was too late, the bale may only have been dried grass, but it probably weighed a quarter of a tonne, and had built up fearsome speed. It thundered past the guards, scattering them like bowling pins, with Sinter and Saker in hot pursuit. The wheel bounced over the threshold, and on to the bridge beyond, sending puffs of dusty grass up into the air as it went.

Further down, they could see the guard post in a frenzy of activity. The tigers had passed through, leaving the guardians cowering inside in fear, but now the tigers had fled into the bamboo forest beyond, and the men were outside, armed, angry and ready. There would be no escape at the end of the bridge. This was the end of the road. Suddenly the answer became clear. Saker charged the straw bale with his shoulder, diverting its path so it headed towards the side of the bridge. In a single bounce, the bale disappeared into the darkness, plunging to the river below.

"JUMP!" Saker yelled at Sinter.

Clasping the box in her arms as if it were the Crown Jewels, Sinter screamed as she sprinted for the edge of the bridge. Saker opened his mouth and joined in her screaming. As the guards ran towards them, rifles and swords drawn and ready, Saker and Sinter leapt into the darkness, knowing that many metres below ran the icy, rampaging whitewater torrent, and surely a freezing death.

EPILOGUE

The Tibetan Buddhist temple sat at the riverside in the foothills of the Himalayas, its buildings coming down to the high watermark that the river would nudge in full spate. The river here was a brilliant turquoise. Even many hundreds of kilometres downstream of the glaciers that gave birth to it, suspended fine sediments in the water stained it with the hue of gemstones. The tumult thundered with purpose, millions of tonnes of water had been raging through here for every minute of recorded time, and would continue to do so long after humanity ceased to be. The river not only provided sustenance and beauty, but reminded the monks who lived in the temple of the passing of time, of their insignificance in the face of the magnitude of the natural world. The simple white plaster stupas had lines of flags between them almost like colourful washing lines. The red, blue, green and yellow flags fluttered in the wind, the air carrying the prayers inscribed on them out into the world. It was midday, morning meditation was over, and the monks were mostly busy sweeping the floors of the buildings, or tending the simple gardens that surrounded the complex. To one side of the temples the novices, clad in red robes, were engaged in debate. One young monk, often no more than six or seven years old, would sit on the ground answering, while another stood over him, bombarding him with questions. The debate was highly ritualised, and as the first monk half-shouted, half-chanted the question, he would leap forward and clap his hands, demanding a response. With near a hundred young lads yelling, leaping and clapping, it was colourful bedlam!

If you'd looked particularly carefully at the older members of the monastery, busy at their chores, you might have noticed that two of them were rather distinct. One was tall and lithe, his hair close cropped like the other monks, but his features distinctly European rather than Tibetan. Another wore the robes of a Buddhist nun, and had her head covered with a scarf, to hide the fact that her hair was long and dark, not shaven like the others.

Saker and Sinter had been there, under the protection of the abbot, for nearly a month. A couple of monks sent to gather water a little after dawn had found them, lying washed ashore as if corpses borne by the flow. What remained of the hay bale that had become their raft was littered about them. They were both unconscious, their faces blue from extreme hypothermia. Sinter still clasped a wooden box to her breast, and her frozen fingers wouldn't release it.

Like all peoples who inhabit the icy roof of the world, the monks knew the mountain mantra: "You're not dead till you're warm and dead." Many of the body's processes – even the heartbeat and breathing – merely go into a kind of coma when subjected to extreme cold. You never give up on a casualty with no vital signs until you've warmed them up, and there is still no response. The two were carried back to the monastery, wrapped in blankets, and the monks played a chanting vigil over their bodies. Young monks were ushered away when they tried to stare into the room at the curious corpses that lay within. And sure enough, as they were gradually warmed, signs of life started to return.

After several days, Sinter had been the first to awaken. The deep, deep cold had cut her to the bones, and she hadn't the energy to lift her head, but she could still ask, "The cubs?"

A beautiful Tibetan face smiled down at her, and a warm hand was placed on her forehead. There was no comprehension, but she could sense that somehow, everything was going to be all right. Saker had woken later that day. He had been in the water longer than Sinter, fighting to get to the hay bale raft, and then finally to clamber on board, and was very close to death. Even now, a month later, he had little feeling in his fingertips and toes, and feared they may never be the same again. On particularly

239

chilly nights, memories of the ice of the river would return to him, and he would sit shivering uncontrollably. The monks would have to restrain him from throwing himself into the blazing fire, so deep, both mentally and physically, was the cold that had taken him that night.

The cubs had fared rather better, insulated in their wooden box even as the hay bale raft had come apart over the rapids. The monks had taken the young cats on with glee, particularly as the tiger was a totem animal for them, its glorious orange, stripy image painted on all the walls and pillars of the temple buildings. The monks fed them, and gave them the freedom of the compound, but made sure to limit the amount of human contact they received, in the hope that someday they could be returned to the wild. If they became too used to human contact at this important stage in their lives, they would not have learned to fear man, and at some later stage might approach people when in need of food. This would inevitably result in the animals getting shot by terrified humans. The abbot was a learned man, and ensured that the cubs were fed without ever seeing that the food was coming from a human source. As Buddhism forbids the killing of another being, they could not countenance killing animals to provide meat for the cubs, but instead had the novices trawling the surrounding hills for recently dead animals that could provide sustenance.

After a month in the care of the temple, the abbot called Sinter and Saker in to his rooms. He wore exactly the same robes as the youngest of the monks, but his shaven head was pitted with liver spots, and his wrinkled face had an air of calm that instantly told of his self-deprecating authority. He was the only person in the monastery who spoke any English, but so far they had managed to get by fine with gestures and smiles.

"So, you are both recovering well now. Soon it will be time for you to return to your own peoples."

The pair bowed to him.

"I have never asked what brought you – or your charges – to our temple. Perhaps it is better that I do not know. But I have sensed something," he paused, then continued. "There is much good in both of you . . . I do not know the path you are seeking, but perhaps it will become clear if you follow these simple words: the greatest achievement is selflessness. The greatest worth is self-mastery. The greatest quality is seeking to serve others. The greatest action is not conforming with the world's ways." With that, he placed his hand first on the head of Sinter, then on Saker. Both felt a tangible sense of well-being flood through them. As they sat back up again, there were tears in their eyes.

"What of the cubs?" Sinter asked.

The abbot smiled. "My initiates will be glad to see them go, they have had their fill of dragging dead deer from the mountainsides!"

He gave an infectious laugh, which didn't seem to fit his beatific manner. "But we will feed them up for another few months, let them become strong, then when the time is right let them go their way. It is not well known if the tiger still prowls these mountains . . . my predecessor sometimes saw the footprints at the riverside. Perhaps we will see them here again."

"So what now?" Sinter asked. "Where does the road take us?"

"Well," said Saker, who had been thinking about it for many days now. "My first move has to be to cross back into India. There is a safe house in one of the slums in Calcutta. There are new identities stored there, money, enough for me to keep running for many years . . . it's bound to be being watched, but I reckon I'll come up with something. And you?"

Sinter looked at him, trying to gauge his thoughts. "I've been thinking I'd like to do something bigger to help the tigers. Maybe I could get involved with a charity or something. I'll have to head back to India first too."

"Maybe we'd best stick together for a little while then," Saker offered, "I don't want you getting in any trouble . . ."

"All the trouble I've ever had in my life has been thanks to you!" she retorted and they both laughed.

"Where are we going to cross the border?" Saker ventured. "We can't go back to the same border post, we'll almost certainly get caught."

"Well, we could always make our way west, through

the mountains. I'd like to see more of this place."

"Before we go, there's one thing we have to do," Saker began carefully. He produced a bottle of dark ink, and a sharpened splinter of bamboo. Sinter raised an eyebrow inquisitively.

By candlelight, Saker screwed up his face as he concentrated on the delicate job in hand. Sinter fought back the urge to cry out in pain. Repeatedly Saker stabbed at the skin on her lower leg, just above her ankle. As he punctured the flesh, he introduced the ink into the wound, where it would be become a permanent tattoo. After an hour or so, he sat back. Sinter sighed with relief, and together they examined his handiwork.

There on her calf, in simple monochrome, was the head of a snarling tigress.

Don't miss book two of

**THE
FALCON
CHRONICLES**

GHOSTS OF THE FOREST

Read on for a preview.

PROLOGUE

The fat man adjusted his belt, opening it one more notch. Any further, and he would have to cut down on the noodles. Either that or buy a new belt. He breathed a little more easily, placed his coffee on the desk, adjusted his $500 silk tie and twisted around on his green leather swivel chair. Before him, the vast window of his office stared out onto a sumptuous lagoon, its pontoons lined with super yachts. The lagoon was manmade; just five years ago the view had been of mangroves, bustling with birds, crocodiles and monkeys. Now it was a marina bustling with the elite of modern Borneo. The swanky office block was the centrepiece of the development, and Amir's office was the penthouse. The building housed both the Malayan environmental protection agency, and also the Malaysian logging industry. Amir was the president of both. Despite the outrage of conservation organisations, the man whose job it was to protect the rainforests of Southeast Asia also gained the most from cutting them down.

Amir didn't have a problem with that. To him it was all about making the most of Malaysia's resources. Places like Britain and Australia had cut down all their forests, who were they to say Malaysia should not do the same? Of course, if he got very, very rich from it, then that would be even better.

It had been a very good week for Amir's bank accounts. Several logging companies were bidding for the right to cut down big chunks of forest. They were going to turn them into palm oil and acacia plantations. Each contract contained a kickback for Amir, and he'd already bought a luxurious house in America and another on the harbour in Sydney. His wasn't the biggest yacht in the marina in front of him, but he was working on that.

Life was pretty good, but it was not perfect. He'd been hit by a flour bomb at the Malayan parliament a few weeks ago. It had been thrown by some greenie lunatic. He'd also had death threats from crazed environmental groups, none of which he took seriously. He'd made front page news in the Straits Times talking about the 'enviro-mentals' or 'bunny huggers', and about how Malaysia would be a global superpower within a decade, by exploiting the 'living gold' of the forests of Borneo.

Today however, something had happened that made his skin clammy with fear.

Amir had come to work that morning as he did every

day, greeted his secretary, walked into his plush office and dropped his briefcase. Then in his regular ritual, he went to get himself a coffee, which he placed on his leather-clad desk. He set to reading his mail, perfectly arranged on his desk above crisply ironed copies of the Financial Times and the Wall Street journal. However, something on top of the mail caught his attention. It was a carving about the size of his thumb, wrought from a piece of fine rainforest wood. He knew instantly from the weight, the espresso coffee colour and swirly grain that this was a rare tropical ironwood. A whole tree could be worth $20,000; more than everyone combined in a native village might earn in a year. He picked it up, admiring the beautiful grain, and the smoothness of the unvarnished carving. Someone had spent hours making this, and taken great care over it. But why would anyone send him a wooden bullet?

Amir reached across to the intercom on his desk; "*Ibu,* come in here please.' Within seconds, his secretary was in the office, pad poised.

"*Ibu,* who sent me this?" he demanded, proffering the bullet between finger and thumb.

"I have no idea, *Bapak,*" she responded, "was it among your letters?"

"No, you know it wasn't, it was here on top of my newspapers!" Amir laughed; surely it was a part of some game from one of his colleagues. His secretary shook her head.

"No, *Bapak*, I put those papers there just a minute ago, and there was nothing else here." Something told him she was telling the truth.

Amir paused, then ushered her out. Alone, he wondered what this could mean. The building had a high-tech surveillance system, armed police, and security cameras everywhere. No one could stroll in, place a wooden bullet on his desk and then just walk out again. How could this have happened? As he pondered, he looked at his newspaper. On top lay a piece of paper with a message. It read:

'*Your actions are destroying the forests the whole planet depends on. We are watching and do not forgive. We are going to take from you everything you value.*'

It was signed, '*the Ghosts of the Forest*'. At first he snorted with derisive laughter. But something about it troubled him. Whoever had walked right into his well-guarded office and placed a bullet on his desk, could as easily have placed a real bullet in his skull. It was a well-chosen warning. He pursed his lips, and his brow furrowed. He turned the carved wooden trinket in his fingers. On the underside, where the firing cap would be in a real bullet, was a symbol. Burned into the wood like a brand was the simple outline of a bird of prey. The brooding head of a Saker falcon.

1

Saker started, heart leaping, his senses on high alert. A demonic screech cut the air, like the scream of a child in terrible pain. Nearby, an explosion of feathers from the frantic wingbeats of fruit doves panicked from their slumber. Every one of Saker's muscles tightened, preparing to leap into flight, yet the faces close to him in the shadows didn't flinch. He forced himself to relax; the noise must surely have been the call of some forest bird, one of the thousands he had yet to learn. Telling himself to chill out, he closed his eyes and drew in a deep, calming breath. The air was so thick with moisture he could taste it. Scents of distant fruiting fig and tamarind were sticky in his nostrils. Above, a full moon was occasionally visible through the tangled tendrils of the jungle canopy. Shafts of white moonlight penetrated the heavy air. It was so bright that it was as if someone had dropped a car out of the sky, and it had found its final resting place up in the treetops, its headlights glaring down on the forest floor. The hunters beneath, perhaps ten of them, stepped around the pools of light, hugging tight to the shadows.

Saker was dressed in the same way as his silent companions; a loincloth around his waist, twisted leather and palm bracelets circling his upper arm and ankles. Dark smears of plant dye across his cheeks and chest served to break up his outline like the nebulous stripes and spots of a clouded leopard, helping him to become one with the night. Around his throat was a wooden amulet carved in the shape of a crocodile. All moved barefoot, toes gently feeling for brittle twigs and dry leaves that might betray a careless step with a crackle or rustle. Each man carried in his hand a three-metre long blowpipe called a *keleput*, cut from a single length of wood and hollowed out with a bone drill. Using this, they could propel a poisoned dart perhaps twenty metres with lethal accuracy. The darts were little more than flimsy toothpicks, carved from the stems of palm fronds, but coated in toxins gathered from the sticky latex of the *tajem* tree. They could kill a monkey in seconds, or stop a man's heart in minutes.

Another odd sound. This time not so blood-curdling. The men in the shadows stiffened, their senses keen. The sound came again; it was the chirrup of a bush cricket's wings rubbing together. Saker knew it was a signal made by the practiced lips of the tribe's front tracker, telling them; 'Stop, listen, there is danger ahead'. Saker squinted, trying to make sense of the darkness. His eyes were already accustomed to the night, but it seemed the tribesmen around him were much more capable, their nocturnal vision like a forest cat's. They could clearly see something he couldn't. After a few seconds concentration, what he thought were distant fireflies became weak electric lights; it was a camp. Civilization! His fingers brushed the wooden handle of the long *Tueh* knife at his hip. His companions had been quiet before, but now they became ghosts of the forest, no more than a memory as they stole through the night.

Abruptly the caverns of the forest came to an end, and before them lay a smouldering field. It was peppered by the sad stumps of ancient ironwood trees, deep furrows showed where clunking yellow machines had dragged away trees that had been growing for centuries. The timber was bound for Malaysian logging mills to make wood chips to line suburban flower borders and rabbit hutches. The logging camp in the centre of the wasteland had been built to last no more than a few weeks. That was all it would take to totally eradicate this patch of forest that had been growing for tens of thousands of years.

The camp was centred around two portacabins, and a ragtag collection of flapping blue tarpaulins. Campfires crackled, and mangy-looking dogs, chickens and a few flea-bitten pigs picked around piles of rubbish in search of scraps. A scratchy stereo blasted out a whining voice, a crude copy of a Western pop song. Saker winced; it sounded as if the singer had been sucking on a helium balloon, and the backing track seemed to have been played on a $10 children's synthesizer. It couldn't have been more out of place against the glorious cicada, frog and cricket orchestra that was the natural soundtrack of the Bornean jungle night.

On the other side of the clearing several vehicles were rusting in the mud, huge, battered Toyota Landcruisers with tyres as tall as a man. There was an industrial digger, and trucks loaded with felled trees as grand in scale and size as the columns on the Parthenon. Each tree was daubed with paint showing where it was felled and where it would be sent. The trunks were four metres in diameter. Saker glanced at one of his companions waiting for the next signal. In the white moonlight, he noticed the trickle of a tear running down the man's cheek. The man looked back at Saker, aware of his gaze. The tribesman made a series of gestures, pointing to the clearing with his thumb, looking up at the sky, then taking the amulet around his neck he rubbed it, and closed his eyes. This place was sacred. It had been a grove where his ancestors had been buried over the centuries. It was one of the last places the treasured ironwood trees had been preserved from the logger's chainsaws. His forefathers were buried here, and their spirits were one with the living wood. Those trees were now stacked on a truck and bound for the sawmill.

His people, the *Penan,* kept no photographs or mementos. They believed that the dead would always live in the forest, watching over their descendants like guardian angels. This was more than a vandalised graveyard. It was as if the outsiders had murdered his family.

Saker felt his muscles tensing again. Without realising it his teeth clenched and adrenalin had started to leak into his blood, quickening his heart rate. The Clan called this sensation 'the rush', the moment of excitement before a kill, when wolves yip and whine with bloodlust, and an assassin's fingertips tingle. They were taught that when they felt the rush, they should breathe deep to quell the adrenalin. Those who didn't might unleash a spear too early, or make rash decisions. The Penan as hunters knew the rush just as well, and doubtless had their own name for it. They had to be cautious. They'd been doing whatever they could to sabotage this plunder of their lands for over a decade now, and the loggers would be ready. They'd be armed with shotguns and possibly even automatic rifles. Anyone who was captured would be shot. Now was not the time to stampede in with a wasted war cry.

They split, moving around the outskirts of the clearing, heading for the monstrous vehicles. Their bare feet squelched in the orange mud; all that remained now that the fragile jungle top soils had been exposed. A tall man had stepped out of the portacabin and into the pool of light beneath an occasionally flickering naked light bulb. He was no more than three steps from Saker. Saker pursed his lips, making the bush cricket chirp that meant; "stop, pay attention". The logger's features were briefly illuminated, and Saker smelled the acidic phosphorous from a struck match. The man had pockmarked swarthy cheeks – scarring from childhood acne – and a wispy moustache. As he breathed out a cloud of perfumed smoke from his *kretek* cigarette, Saker's nostrils registered the sweet smell of cloves. He could have reached over and plunged his knife up to the hilt in the man's chest, but this was against the ways of the peaceful Penan. Saker knew that if he did anything violent, he would wake up alone in the forest tomorrow. His companions would have gone, leaving not so much as a footprint to prove they had ever existed. Saker merged into the background, swaying imperceptibly in the gentle wind like a praying mantis, to mimic the slight movement of the trees. Saker's eyes were already adjusted to the darkness, pupils wide to absorb as much light as possible, while the man had just stepped out of the artificial light, leaving him with no night vision. Saker was as good as invisible to him. The logger sucked the last of his cigarette and dropped the stub, crushing it under the heel of his cowboy boot. He turned, and walked back inside.

With the threat gone, the Penan glided through the camp, intent on quiet destruction. Petrol caps were untwisted, and sugar poured into the fuel tanks. Tyres were slashed and fan belts sliced. The chainsaws that bit so cruelly into the flesh of the sacred trees had their chain-links sprung and starting cords cut. The larger machines that could deal out the most deadly terror on the forest received special attention. The Penan had seen their first motor vehicles less than a decade before, but had quickly learned how best to paralyse them.

No matter how satisfying it was to see hydraulic fluid spilling into the mud, or to pull out electric wires, the Penan knew their actions were useless. The loggers had the

Malaysian government behind them. They might stop the diggers rolling for a few days, but parts would soon be shipped, and the chainsaws would rage again. All it would take would be one satellite phone call… Saker's attention was caught by a long aerial sticking up out of one of the portacabins. It was a radio antenna. Almost all of these logging camps had portable satellite dishes that enabled them to keep in touch with the outside world, but the dense ceiling of forest often cut out the signal. This camp was relying on old-fashioned radio technology! If Saker could sabotage that system, the loggers would have to walk to the nearest town, and that might take two or three days. It would certainly slow their recovery. Saker crept across the mud towards the light. There was an urgent snort from behind him, the alarm call of a proboscis monkey made by one of the Penan, trying to catch his attention. Saker knew the message behind the sound; "you're straying from the plan! Don't do anything stupid!" He didn't even glance back.

The aerial was on top of one of the makeshift buildings. Saker climbed up using the windowsills as footholds, and slid over the roof. He moved with great caution, aware that the plastic ceiling was taut as a drum, and footfalls would sound like a boom to the people inside. The aerial was attached to a large black box to keep the workings safe from jungle rain. Saker used the tip of his knife to unscrew one side of the box and pull it away. Inside was a morass of wires he didn't know how to operate, but did know how to sabotage. He reached inside, grabbed a handful, and pulled.

It was as if he had grabbed hold of an electric cow fence with both hands. The shock threw him bodily backwards onto the roof with an involuntary shriek. He rolled straight to his feet, prepared to leap off the roof and run. Instantly a commotion started inside the portacabin, and within seconds, he found himself staring down into blinding torchlight. This time the tables were turned, it was the logger who had light on his side. The man shouted at him in a language Saker didn't understand. Behind the glare of the torch, Saker could just make out the sheen of a gun-barrel. He slid down and dropped to the mud.

The whole mission had been compromised because of him. The Penan would have melted into the forest by now, and he might never find them again.

The pockmarked man gesticulated with the rifle, barking questions Saker couldn't understand. Saker's mind screamed, searching for a way out. He certainly couldn't count on mercy. These were lawless, hard men. Unless Saker found a way out, they would kill him and dump his body where it would never be found. The loggers couldn't comprehend why anyone would want to live in the forest. For them it was hot, wet, humid, thick with biting bugs, a miserable hell that made all their equipment and clothing rust and rot. But they hadn't seen the wonders that Saker had; hidden waterfalls hung with hundred-year old pepper vines, the haunting songs of gibbons echoing over a misty valley as the sun began to rise. And most of all, they knew nothing of the orang utan, the old man of the forest. To Saker and the Penan, it was a totem animal. Our own image, clothed in umber fur, tranquilly munching fruit in the treetops. The forests had to remain, or the orang utan would fade away, and take with it a big part of our souls. It was the orangs that had drawn Saker to Borneo. He hoped that he might be able to do something to help the forests, to help the apes.. But the loggers were city-folk, hated the forest, and cared nothing for the orang utan. Furthermore as they were getting paid per tree they cut down, the efforts of the saboteurs took money from their pockets.

As his mind raced, his eye was caught by the glimmer of naked metal behind the shoulder of his adversary. It was one of the Penan - he'd come back! It was Leysin, the man he had seen shedding a tear earlier. His long *Tueh* knife was drawn, and it was clear he intended to plunge it into the back of the logger. Saker couldn't let that happen. Penan culture had no truck with killers, Leysin would be made an outcast. Saker raised his hands in the universal gesture of surrender, then stepped towards his captor. The pockmarked man raised the rifle from his hip to his shoulder, clearly telling Saker to stay exactly where he was. The boy nodded, and spoke in a placating voice; "I'm really sorry man, I just have friends who live here that's all." It didn't matter what he said, he was just buying time. "Come on, you don't want to waste bullets on me!"

Leysin crept forward, knife held high. Saker had to act. He snapped his hand out, and grabbed the tip of the rifle barrel, pulling it towards himself, then rolling his whole body in a balletic move down the length of the gun towards the Malaysian. When his back lay flat against the gun, Saker jacked his elbow into the throat of his captor, who doubled up gasping for breath. Saker then took his legs from under him with a leg sweep, like a farmer reaping corn with a scythe. The rifle, and its owner dropped unceremoniously into the mud. Saker and Leysin ran for the shadows.

As they scampered over the exposed roots and tree stumps, shouting rang out, and then several 'cracks', and the whiz of bullets about their ears. It was panic fire, the loggers couldn't see them in the darkness and were shooting blindly. Almost at the trees, Saker ducked as another round fizzed overhead. Then the welcoming arms of the jungle, cloaked him in its dark blanket. But he was alone. Where was Leysin? Squinting back towards the bedlam of the camp, Saker made out a shadowy figure struggling to get up from the dirt. Saker turned and ran back towards him. Torch beams sliced the darkness, but the loggers were scared to venture into the jungle at night. Saker grabbed the Penan, who lay breathing heavily, and dragged him towards safety, as more shots rang out and angry voices screamed vengeance. Leysin could still keep himself upright, but only just. Saker propelled him forwards, taking one arm over his shoulder and putting his hand round Leysin's waist. He could feel warm sticky blood around Leysin's midriff; at least one of the bullets had found its mark. They stumbled off, the Penan hunter groaning with every step.

AUTHOR'S NOTE

This story of Saker, Sinter and the Clan is one that has been going round in my head now for many years, and though their adventures may be a fantasy, the realm I've set them in is very much real. The north of India and the Himalaya are to me one of the most special places in the world. I've spent many months here on expeditions, and the descriptions of the places the young pair find themselves in are all drawn from the pages of my diaries. I've tried to evoke the flavour of the place as much as possible, but that will never be entirely possible, as it's somewhere that kind of defies description in words. It's a place of great contrasts, where the world's highest mountains can make a human being feel impossibly tiny, and flood-prone lowlands and deserts can seem to bake the soul. Here great beauty sits alongside great poverty, spiritual spectacles and unimaginable colour battle with the greyness of pollution, the dizzying scents of the world's finest foods, spices and perfumes is occasionally tainted by the odour of a rotting dog corpse in the gutter, and natural wonders are tempered by terrible environmental degradation. It's a place that anyone with a lust for travel, and a desire to understand humanity should try to go to at some point in their lives.

As for the plight of the tiger depicted in these pages, well, I really wish this was fiction. However every word that's written here about tigers is true. I've seen first hand the troubles that face this majestic beast in Tibet, China, Nepal, India, Bhutan and Southeast Asia, and it genuinely breaks my heart. While working with the big cat conservation group Pantera, conservationist Alan Rabinowitz (probably the most inspirational man I've ever met) asked me; "if we can't save tigers, the most majestic, dramatic and loved of all animals, then what hope is there for the rest of the planet's wildlife?" His words have stayed with me, and very much inspired me to write this book. However, I think it's really important that this is an adventure story in which tigers take their part, rather than a morality play. My sincere hope is that my readers will be swept along by the journey, but perhaps leave a little more aware of the traumas that face tigers, and may choose to do something about it. For anyone wishing to find out more, Pantera.org is an excellent place to start.

For a lifetime of wild adventures …

Steve Backshall
London, January 2012